I Do Not Apologize for My Position on Men

A Collection by Rae Wilde

Manuscript Copyright 2024 Rae Wilde
Logo Copyright 2020 Off Limits Press
Cover design by Sofia Ajram
Interior Design by W. Dale Jordan
Edited by W. Dale Jordan and Others

This is a work of fiction. All characters and events portrayed in this work are fictitious and any resemblance to real people or events is purely coincidental.

No part of this book may be reproduced, stored in a retrieval system, or transmitted in any form or by any means, electronic, mechanical, photocopying, recording, or otherwise, without the prior written permission of the author.

TABLE OF CONTENTS

Introduction i

Part I: 1

John List Would Like to Cancel His Subscription to Omaha Steaks 1

Rusalnaya 9

I Am Not The Ghost You Wanted 15

Giltiné 23

Between Her Teeth 29

A Fine Wife, Indeed 41

I Gave My Heart to a Hurricane 51

Eyes Open, Knees Apart for the End of the World 57

A Curse in the Midnight Zone 63

Backseat Driver 71

Write My Eulogy On The Gloryhole Bathroom Stall 83

Part II: 93

Mulberry Silk 95

Common Oleander 111

Of Ash and Soot 121

Gemma Prepared to Dive 129

Part III: 145

Survive the Essex 147

   Lance The Whale 153

Get in the Whale Boat 161

Stay on the Island 165

Let it Go 167

Head to the Marquesas 171

Head to the Easter Island 175

Epigraph 181

Content Warnings 183

For the women who cut bangs or bleached their hair or let it go gray or got the promotion or stayed at home or took a while to leave him or her or them or played sports or went tanning or vacationed at Disney or have never been or call their mother every day or wish they had that kind of mom or did not recognize themselves at 2am in that bar bathroom mirror or asked their teachers about extra credit or the horse girls or DIY queens who cried quietly when what they really wanted to do was scream.

I am just like you.

Introduction

By the time you finish this marvelous collection you will see the grand absurdity in the fact that a man is writing its foreword. For Rae Wilde, the world is overfilled with pain and trauma and problems, and for each of these, there is a man who fills its shape. And though I am counted among men in the world, believe deeply in the good work men are capable of doing for and with those around them when they decide to do so, this small but powerful volume makes clear the challenge every single man presents to the whole sum of people sharing the world with them.

Men love to worship other men, are easily drawn into the personality cult of the 'strong man' or the ridiculous 'alpha male' mentality, and certainly as a collective are much more selfish than we are willing to admit. Men's self-beliefs, their nature, their hearts, all of them singular to each man and each man directed by those three instruments which comprise their internal compass.

Rae Wilde wants men to bear witness to a singular fact-the compass inside the heart of every living man is broken.

As a man, as a writer, I can make no case against her argument.

While this collection features men, it is certainly not *about* men. This work is about deeply imperfect human beings living in an imperfect world. A world overflowing with passion. How they interact with the world and how the world interacts with them in ways that are shocking and violent, filled with malice. That malice suffuses the whole narrative threadline of each and every shattering story within these pages.

I have my favorites.

You will too.

It's a rare thing, more rare than most of us would like to admit, to find such unflinching human nakedness in the artistry of storytelling today. Not of the bodily kind, but the sheer genuine baring of every scar and infirmity and near every shade of harm worn on the invisible flesh of the heart. Rarer still for a collection to so simply state, "Here I am. I am as my choices and time and circumstances have made me. And I do not apologize for my position on men."

Though the title implicitly directs itself as a shaft toward the beating heart of all men, I would encourage them to disabuse themselves of ego. Remove vanity's panoply. Bravely bear your naked breast and allow each and every arrow to pierce you. Let those arrows sink feather-deep into your misaligned form.

The author has come wearing nothing but the truth.

I wonder if you can do the same. If you can see all the strength the laying down of arms requires.

I hope you can.

This collection is not *about* men. How could it be?

How could such a grand thing be relegated to so little a topic?

It is my observed opinion: Rae Wilde is one of the best living writers working in the world today. And for those of you who are only reading her work now, at this moment in time, not yet having read anything else of hers or seen what is to come next, I have good news for you. Perhaps the best.

This is only the beginning. And from this little capstone bridging the arch of the first passage of her career, you will see that she's only going to build further. Reach higher.

Up and up and up, far beyond the place where the heat of critical review junctions with mercurial nature of the broad audience the world over.

This collection is the unmistakable viewing of a writer soaring and succeeding, rising above the Icarus Point.

C.S. Humble
Sugar Land, TX
April, 2024

Part I:

11 Ways to Die Alone

John List Would Like to Cancel His Subscription to Omaha Steaks

Published by *Ghoulish Tales*, July 2023

"That's right, a family vacation," John said, lowering his hand from the dial. As the AC kicked on, he cringed. Sixty degrees would be unthinkable under any other circumstance. Who would ever need a home that cold? The bill would be outrageous.

The whirr of a nearby vent obscured the voice of the receptionist on the other end, but he thought he made out something like *winter breaks* and *make-up assignments*.

"Thank you, ma'am."

"Of course, Mr. List. Enjoy your holiday."

The tangled cord spun and wrapped around itself as he placed the phone in its proper resting place. From the mantle, a portrait leered. He pulled the notepad from his pocket, drawing a single line through *Call the school* and tucked it safely inside his coat, the next item, *Photos*, top of mind.

John took a high step to reach his duffle bag, avoiding the soiled carpet. Slinging the strap over one arm and sliding open the zipper, he ushered the portrait inside. Making his way from room to room, collecting images of himself as he went, it struck him that every picture captured the same vacant expression. A bit winded when he climbed to the second floor, he was suddenly relieved to feel the icy breath of the air conditioning on the back of his neck.

Good planning, John, he assured himself.

A void in his stomach grumbled. The bank had taken longer than expected, he'd had to stop at the field, and then the whole mess with his eldest boy... His shoulder ached in the socket. John was not the young man he once was. He stretched his arm from one side to the other. Had he dislocated it? It didn't matter. He had a plan.

And dinner was thirty minutes past due.

Making his way through the children's rooms and back down the stairs, he hoped Helen hadn't eaten all the ham, that Alma had secured the twist tie on the bread so it wasn't stale, *again*. Framed photos clanked against one another in the duffle, but he knew the cash beneath would provide enough cushion to keep the glass from breaking, and when he reached the kitchen, he lowered the bag onto Patricia's empty chair.

There were a few slices of ham left. The bread was only partially stale, and as John munched the sandwich, he once again checked over his list.

Omaha Steaks.

The next delivery was due a week from Sunday, two New York strips and a porterhouse. He couldn't have them rotting on the porch. The kitchen phone had an extra long cord, and though he usually thought it was gauche, John set the receiver face up on the table and placed the call on speaker so he could finish his lunch and remain, for the most part, on schedule.

She answered on the second ring.

"Omaha Steaks, delivering premium meats since 1917. How might I help you?"

"Hello, this is Mr. List and I'm calling to cancel my subscription."

"Oh!" Her voice lost none of its cheeriness. "I am so sorry to hear, Mr. List. Was the last delivery," clicking in the background, "on September 21st not to your satisfaction?"

"It's not that." John moved a bite of ham, smothered in a too large bead of mayo, to the back of his mouth. "We're going out of town, you see."

"How lovely. A trip for the holidays?"

"Yes." John sucked down a swallow of milk. "The whole family will be gone, so there will be no one here to receive the package." His eyes wandered over the center of the ballroom. "I hate to think of it rotting."

"Well, Mr. List, I can put your mind at ease. No need to cancel, we can delay the delivery. When do you expect to return?"

"That's the thing–" John cleared his throat, mucous already flaring up from the dairy. "We're moving."

A beat passed.

"After your vacation?"

"After our vacation." John stood and rinsed the empty glass under the faucet. Noticing a rusty smudge at his wrist, he wiped it away with the excess moisture. It must have hid beneath his cuff, but there was no excuse for sloppiness. John would need to be more careful.

"Moving is quite the undertaking, Mr. List. Wouldn't it be nice to have one less thing to worry about while you're unpacking boxes? We can transfer your subscription, if you give us the new address, I can update our system and change the delivery date–"

She was talking fast now, customer service training no doubt kicking in, so John had to cut her off. "I'm not interested, thank you."

"Perhaps you'd like to check with your wife?" More clicking keys. "Won't the kids miss steak dinners? We have you down as a family of five."

"Six." John let the ire shoot through him and waft away. "My mother has a room in the attic."

"How good of you, John, taking care of your mother. May I call you John?"

John shifted. He hadn't expected the flush of warmth in her tone. "Sure."

"Well, John, would you like to check with them before we cancel? Just to be sure?"

Again, John's eyes passed over the ballroom. "There's no need."

"I understand. I'm going to go ahead and transfer you to my supervisor to complete the cancellation. Hold please."

A cheesy instrumental version of an Eagles song–John couldn't remember which one–gave him an idea. While he waited, he went to the radio in the ballroom, setting it to play an AM Christian station at full volume.

"...crouched, waiting to steal, lie, and devour."

"John List?" This voice had syrupy notes of southern sweetness.

"Damnation awaits those who stray from the path..."

"Yes!" he called over the recorded sermon, scuttling back from the neighboring room.

"...Mercy shall be saved for those deemed righteous."

"My colleague tells me you'd like to cancel your subscription."

John cradled the phone using his body, his best attempt to block the background noise. He cleared his throat. "That's right."

"She says you and your *whole* family are going away, and then moving." John couldn't place the strange inflection on the word.

So, he just said, "That's right."

"You know," the woman let her breath crackle over the line, "sometimes I get calls from men who think they want to cancel their order."

"...to inherit the kingdom of God..."

Light refracted off the gun's barrel. He'd laid it there, still hot, and now the evening sun seemed to wink at him as it poured through the blinds and bounced off the black metal.

"But they really just want to reduce the quantity. Say… from family of five–six, you said! To just one."

"Abraham so trusted in the Lord…"

John mindlessly rubbed his fingertips together where the burn interrupted his usual swirl pattern. "Just one." He'd been too quick to pick up the spent casing.

"Faith! Pure faith!"

"Our cuts are the highest quality," she continued, "but our New York strips are nearly a pound, our porterhouses more like a pound and a half. That's a lot of meat, John. Don't you think?"

John's thought, *too much, too heavy*, came out as a *hmmm*.

"You're not the only one. So many men think they want a family portion, think they *should be able to handle* that much meat. But it's too much sometimes, isn't it, John?"

John let the silence hang there as he considered it. Hard as he tried, it had been too much.

"Good men, capable providers, even…"

She continued but John could only focus on the scent of iron, the relentless nagging, the beast that was sin moving ever closer to his children, his legacy, the threat that crescendoed into a scheduled series of blasts, and now the quiet—the delicious quiet made thicker by the hum of the AC.

"So, do you?"

A flush of embarrassment. John was meticulous; he didn't like missing things. He didn't like repeating things. A flash of his eldest boy, grunting, uniform stained. "Do I what?"

"Do you think reducing your order, rather than canceling it, might be the way to go?"

When was the last time John enjoyed a steak? *Really* enjoyed it, without the press of eyes across the table?

"As I said, we can change the delivery address. Maybe somewhere out west? It's really no trouble at all."

"Out west?" John had a vague idea of where he would go, but wanted to hear out this woman, this woman who seemed to understand him more than Helen, certainly more than Alma or the kids.

"I hear lovely things about Denver. We can hold your order 'til you're settled in there. You can just give me a call back. Wendy. You call and ask for Wendy."

"That's kind of you, Wendy." When was the last time a woman had taken the time to be kind to him?

"The cold is important, John."

A shiver crept over his shoulder blades. "The cold?"

"Our meat is stored in a deep freezer to ensure freshness. Without the cold, it would really be a mess."

John smirked. He let his gaze pass over the windows: firmly shut, blinds closed. He let his mind wander and find the image of rotted meat, a green, iridescent sheen around clusters of pearl-sized eggs, maggots nestling into layers of rancid tissue, making a home there. Then he thought of clean cuts, frozen and meticulously packaged so not a drop of blood leaked through, the blue hue of freezer lighting, the neat, chilled stack in the ballroom. "Yes, the cold is important."

"Very important."

John eyed the duffle bag, the duffle bag containing his fresh start.

"It's a long trip to Denver."

An undisturbed steak did sound nice, a steak alone in Denver.

"You know what I'd like to do for you, John?"

"What's that?"

"I'd like to open you a new account, for *just one* under a new name. Something that will blend in Denver–or anywhere, really. Something like Bob... Bob Clark. What do you say?"

"Bob Clark." John had thought of Roger Hammons, but this was even better, less remarkable. "It's a strong name."

"Oh yes." More clicking. "A strong name for a man strong enough to start over, and not cheat himself out of the finer things in the process. Are two weeks enough?"

"Are two weeks enough for what?"

"To settle in Denver. I'll schedule you for a call back in two weeks, Mr. Clark."

It was silly.

John knew that.

She didn't want to lose a customer, likely worked on commission. She didn't know. She had no special affection toward him, but still... the way she rolled Mr. Clark off her tongue... For the first time in a long time, John felt less alone.

"How will you get my number?"

"Hah!" A light smack of flesh on flesh, and John pictured the woman slapping her forehead. "Of course, how silly of me. You'll call me then. This number is just fine, you can ask for Wendy."

"Yeah, you said that."

"Do we have a plan, Mr. Clark?"

John pulled a ballpoint pen from the kitchen junk drawer. "It's a plan."

"Excellent, Bob. I look forward to speaking with you soon." A gentle click and John walked the phone back to its resting place on the wall. Once more, he pulled the notebook from his pocket, this time penning a new entry.

November 23, call Omaha Steaks: Wendy

Below, he scrawled the customer service number.

John pushed the crumbs from his plate into the sink drain and rinsed the dish, drying his palms on the hand towel. Lifting the gun from the counter, he switched the safety on and tucked it into the duffle bag still resting on Patricia's empty chair.

Stepping over the heap of bodies in the ballroom, John took one last look at his massive home, running through the list.

Bank. Check.
Gas. Check.
Cancel milk, mail, newspaper. Check.
Pastor's letter. Check.
Lights on. Close blinds. Check.
Turn down AC. Check.
Call the school. Check.
Photos. Check.
Omaha Steaks. Check.

Turning up each foot, he examined the soles of his shoes–no blood. With a sigh, he let himself out, locking the door behind him. Duffle bag secured in the trunk, John–*No*, he reminded himself, *Bob*–flipped the ignition, and set course west. To Denver.

Where a quiet steak dinner was waiting.

Rusalnaya

Published by *Seize the Press*, October '22

I wake in June, free from my former self. Rhythmic beating of the tides have washed away most of the troublesome details from *before*: my name, how I came to be, relations. Scrubbed and purged by my mother the sea, I stretch upon a bed of shifting sands. Glowing orbs twinkle through the otherwise impenetrable darkness, a blanket of nautical stars through the midnight zone. Quiet lays thick in the deep, and if not for the hunger driving me, I think I'd settle, plunge what's left of my toes into sugar sand, and let the water's gentle sway rock me back into slumber.

Alas, my craving wins out. I push off from the bottom, a flurry of disturbed seabed rising around me like a waterspout. I don't see it, but feel the grit tickle my edges, burrow into my rotted flesh. Sunlight begins to penetrate the black and I see the full truth of myself. As I kick, chunks of me cling to bone. Strips of gray flesh wave like tattered flags. Some snap off, roots too gnarled away by saltwater to hold their grip. But it's no matter, the bits of me that spiral back down to the deep will feed my lessers: sharks and squid that scan the bottom looking for tasty morsels. I am pleased to be of service to them.

My billowing tendrils of hair collect kelp in the ascent like so much jewelry. The mirror surface of the Adriatic sea, *Adriana*, my mother, welcomes me with my own warped reflection. I think, before I crack the surface, of how beautiful I have become, how powerful. The moment I breach, I'm gifted with a name. Eleanor. A tad troublesome in my mouth, so I shorten it. Ella. This is the name I will give them.

There's no pain as my eyes adjust to the sun. Adriana collected my pain in her generous waves, ushered it to distant shores. Only the hunger remains. Atop white caps I travel toward the smattering of green in the East. What was a splash of color becomes raised tree tops, becomes the baked clay roofs of a town surrounded by forest, becomes a weather worn dock, a port speckled with fishing vessels. The men don't see me as I reach the shallows, too distracted by stringing banners and lugging barrels of spirits.

My skeletal feet find purchase on the rocky shoreline, and my head and neck clear the water. As droplets slip from emerging shoulders, their luster is restored. Smooth skin stretches over my chest and arms, and my young, hollow body glistens in the daylight. I trudge up to shore, waves sloshing about my knees, stirring sea foam in my wake, and my bodice clutches at my breasts, once again full beneath my burgundy skirts, silken and untattered as the day they were tailored. My hair is a tangled mess of curls. The tips lick my elbows as Adriana kisses me goodbye.

I will see you again soon, I whisper, though only in my mind.

A fisherman has taken notice of me. My red skirts and youth are stark against the gray stone and lapping waves. He hovers above a crab trap, rope in hand, observing me like a specter. I let him watch as my bare feet meet the cobblestone road. Painted signs adorn vendor tables on either side of the main street. *La Serenissima* is painted blue and pink and yellow by ribbons extended from balconies and affixed to clothing lines. I sense my sisters amongst the bustling crowd, hungry as I am and hidden from view. Our name is whispered by a thousand tongues, *Rusalka*. It is their mentioning that wakes us, ignites our hunger, draws us from the sea. Each June we answer their call, and each year they call again, like fireflies to the flames of their own misfortune.

We needn't consult one another. We each will do what is bidden, what we are driven to do, as soon as the sun dips below the mountainous horizon, and the men have swallowed much wine and ale. I wander and wander until it begins, listening to strange beings talk of strange things, of donkeys and childbirth and weddings. A woman crunches green apple in her mangled teeth as a gray bearded man leans too close to listen, gets bits of fruit spit onto his mustache while she chomps. Their horrid flirtation sparks my lust, a sweet reminder of my purpose. The festival, Rusalnaya, is held in our honor, and we honor them by accepting their sacrifice.

Finally it is time. The street is bathed in orange glow as the sun nods its fiery head.

His chin is foamy with warm ale. His tan pants grip his calves. He is yours. Find him.

The wind speaks to me, and my craving becomes so deep and wide I think it might tear me open. I scan the crowd and my eyes lock upon a salt and pepper man with a silver mug to his lips. He pulls me to him. I dodge children spinning tops, push aside a stray dog begging for scraps, duck beneath a fallen streamer. My pulse, or something like one, thrums at my temple. I am all fire and craving. He spots me, his glare tight to my bosom. For this I cannot blame him. It is his nature, and this is mine. My lashes flutter and I pass him, though my head turns over my shoulder so he is bidden to follow. Down an alley I go, away from the noise and chatter of the busy town.

Rapturous sounds of folly dampen in thickening fog as I wind through back alleys that stink of fish bellies and rotted lettuce. His steps are close behind me.

Yes, follow.

My loins ache with desire, my belly a vacuous hole. Through the damp air, I see my mother, Adriana, lapping the shore with her greedy tongue. I turn to my man once again, show him my teeth, my curled lip invitation. His pace quickens, and finally the breaking of gentle waves on the rocky shore overtakes the jolly of the now distant festival.

Adriana speaks, *Bring him to me.*

I will! I will!

The tide swirls about my bare feet and finally I stop walking and turn to face him. I say nothing as his boots splash into the tide pool. When his calloused hands catch on my silks, I don't move away. The pressure about my hips only deepens my lust as I take a single step toward the sea. He thinks naught of it, stepping forward to meet me, to clutch at the strings of my corset, untangle them behind my back. I hear my labored breaths, toss my head backward and gaze into the glorious night. He strips me of my dress, tossing it to the shallows, leaving only my pale bodice to reflect the moonlight. We are at the precipice now.

I step backward and step again. He nearly trips over himself to regain his hold on me, and my passion stirs between my thighs, shoots like lightning through my emptied chest and into my fingertips. Waist deep now, I am feral with lust. Desirous lightning dances about my palms, invisible but deadly as my mother sea. When he reaches betwixt my legs, I feel his fingernail scrape bone, and a flash of recognition alights his irises.

"Speak my name," I whisper.

He is frozen as a rat in a glue trap.

"I—I don't…" He trembles.

"Ella is my name."

I yank his arms round my body, the contact ecstasy on my skin above water. Only beneath the depths does my true form show: my mottled flesh hanging in chunks, bits flaking off and nibbled by passing silver fishes.

The crescendo builds, threatening as rolling thunder.

"Speak my name," I command.

"Ella." His grown throat emits the voice of a frightened child. He's weak within my grasp, impotent as a flopping fish.

"My true name."

His quivering jaw hangs open, and the word ekes out. "Rusalka."

I plunge his head beneath the surf, stand square over him with legs parted. The bubbles from his underwater pleas caress my most sensitive places. The crescendo builds. I thrust my hands beneath the water, wriggle my fingers about his underarms, his ribcage. Demented laughter spills from his drowning mug. His wide eyes beg for mercy beneath the waterline, but I tickle and tickle, pulling every bubble of air from his lungs. Delicious pressure from the rising air is a generous lover. My fingers work him and work him, and the crescendo builds. I toss my head back, unable to contain my moans. They escape my full lips like prayers to the oldest gods. At the brink now, I cast my eyes to the hovering moon, and at last his spirit leaves him in a flurry of tiny bubbles, pushing me over the edge of craving into rapturous delight. I shriek. Filled. Sated. Pleasure overtakes me like a torrential storm.

I release my grip on him and let my hands glide around my goosed chest, my nipples pressing against my bodice, and wave after wave of exquisite pleasure rocks my gifted body. I don't know how long I delight in the aftershocks, but when I regain myself, his corpse floats face down in the shallows, already beginning to bloat.

I feel my sisters drawing their targets from the crowd, pulling them toward the beach. I have more decency than to intrude, so I slip beneath the surface, smooth and silent as an eel. Adriana calls me deeper. Happy to oblige, I swim, no need of breath, the black sea stripping away my temporary flesh. I find a cozy spot in the dark deep, beside a coral formation in the shape of a cave. The sand here is fine and smooth, and the bones of my fingers burrow easily beneath it. I turn and dig my way in like a ray, and the sea floor happily accepts me as one of its own. Faintly, I see the smiling moon through the bucking, mirror surface. She lulls me into a dreamless sleep, heavy enough to last a year.

I Am Not The Ghost You Wanted

Published by Off Limits Press in *Make Your Presence Known*, March 2024

Brinn stirs the macaroni until the heat's burned too much liquid from the sauce. It congeals, climbing up the side of the pan, spreading itself in clumps over soggy noodles.

"I'll go shopping tomorrow," she says, spooning matching portions into matching Target bowls. I take my seat across from her at our scarred kitchen table, stare into the goop as she takes her first bite. Too-soft pasta and too-chunky sauce squelch between her molars. Brinn doesn't take care anymore; but she still serves me a portion, out of habit, out of hope.

I am not the ghost you wanted.

"Looks good," I say. My tone does little to cover the lie. Perhaps I too have stopped taking care.

"It's not," she says with a scowl. "You remember what good food looks like, don't you?"

A little barb. More will come, if it continues like this.

"I remember." I shift in my seat. The wooden legs don't creak for me. My tattered clothes drape around deep lacerations in my chest, the memory of glass shards glistening in just the right light.

"Try a bite," Brinn says. She says it every night.

I stare into the yellow mess. Brinn hopes if I can eat, that'll mean I'm not dead. If I'm not dead, I can leave. "No, thank you."

She grunts, shoveling spoonfuls of the slop into her mouth hole rapidfire.

***

It was a quirky project, showing up with rake and trowel and tomato seedlings. She slipped into a denim jumper that barely covered her nipples. She knew it, smirking when she caught my gaze drifting downward. Sunlight dappled through the sea grape tree, our cloth gloves stained black by rich soil. Brinn tucked those unruly strands behind my ear, the bed nearly planted. My flesh vibrated with the possibilities between us.

"You can never, ever leave me," she said.

"What if I die?" I said cheekily, testing her.

"Swear you'll haunt me." She didn't miss a beat, stare unwavering as a dragonfly dipped and darted between us.

I stabbed the trowel into turned earth. "I swear."

Brinn giggled, clear and crisp and joyful, a sound that could drive a nightingale to jealous madness.

"I will love you forever."

We'd only just met.

***

Brinn dumps my portion in the trash. I watch from my seat, but also from a spot near the sink, and just beside the pantry. In every view accessible to me, she scowls. A hunk of cheese sauce gloms onto the garbage bag's thin plastic and falls deeper, crushing a napkin beneath.

Our love is curdled.

"I'm going to bed," she says without looking over her shoulder. She climbs the stairs and my numbness is broken by a flash of envy when the top step groans under her weight.

"Goodnight."

Sleep is her only respite from me, and ghosts don't sleep.

***

I packed a duffle bag, but in my excitement, forgot a toothbrush.

"You can use mine," Brinn said with a smile. The sun had kissed her cheeks and nose with pleasant pink. Her freckles darkened, eyes brightened. Marco Island, usually a crotchety town of Republican retirees, bored and useless, expanded wide enough to hold young love. It was too hot under the covers, our sunburns radiating warmth. I used the excuse to shed my t-shirt and sleep shorts. Brinn didn't need one to shed hers.

She slipped beneath the hotel-white comforter, burying her face between my thighs, teasing me with little flicks of her tongue. Her phone buzzed on the nightstand. She stroked my entrance. Blue light invaded our dark, cozy space. I turned my face away from the intrusion, tried to force myself to focus on the sensation of her: the heat of her hands clutching my hips, the coolness of her breath falling over my wet center—

Her phone buzzed again.

Unease stole my attention. I told myself it was paranoia. I pushed away the feeling. I faked it, flipped her onto her back, and lost myself in the act of service.

We'd been together eight weeks.

***

Brinn tosses and turns. I see it from my spot on the couch downstairs. Her little snores that once were charming now drive away my chance of peace in these quiet hours. The front door calls to me, and I answer, as I do every night. The thrill of fleeting hope snakes through me as I place my hand on the knob, the coppery finish dulled by my translucent presence.

It turns. The door swings open easily, but beyond it, static. Like an old T.V. screen after the network signed off. It's hard, dense, trapping me in my spot. The flicker of hope dies. It's died one hundred and eighty-two times. And yet, every night since I died, I've come to the door. Every night, I've wanted to escape.

I slam it shut, not caring if I wake Brinn. The force rattles the dresser that shares the wall. Brinn remains sleeping. Curiosity leads me to open the dresser drawer. A stack of board games: chess, Shoots and Ladders, Life. The irony's not lost on me. At the bottom of the stack, something dusty.

Ouiji, it reads.

***

Phone buzzing turned to screen shielding turned to unexplained, longer than usual nights out.

"Since I moved in, you've just seemed—"

"You're smothering me!" Brinn's cheeks flushed angry scarlet, her eyes wide with impatience.

"I'm sorry, I just want—"

"Give me some space." Brinn threw herself up the stairs.

My heart pounded and tears flooded my vision. There was someone else. I knew there was someone else. But I didn't want to catch her. I wanted to work it out. Her door– our door–slammed, rattling the bookcase in the hall. I phoned Lidia. It was eight p.m. She'd be done with her shift. She'd pick me up. I'd vent. Brinn would have some time. She'd calm down.

We'd been together four months.

***

I remove the games carefully, reverently. I might've mocked Brinn for being superstitious when I was alive, but now the prospect of communicating with someone, anyone else is too tantalizing to resist. I free the board and lay it out flat on the coffee table. Squinting to read the tiny printed instructions, I gather there's not much to the game: place the planchette with a light hold, ask your questions, summon the dead. Easy.

My fingers rest on the wooden planchette, cheaply printed numbers, letters, *yes*, and *no* mocking me from the folding board. I think of calling my mother. She might offer some comfort, but more likely she'd comment on my haggard appearance. I think of my grandmother, but I barely knew her. It's hard being young and dead. My friends are all living.

I remember Lidia.

***

The scent of tequila rolled off Brinn in thick waves.

"Just go, if that's what you want!"

"I—" My voice hitched. Angry red dots mottled my arms, an embarrassing effect of my strong emotion.

"Go ahead, call up your little savior." Brinn laughed, all contempt, no joy.

Tears rolled down my cheeks. I swallowed what I wanted to say, knowing it would come out broken. I grabbed my bag as Brinn ascended the stairs, unable to even give me the pleasure of knowing she'd watch me leave. Cool night air greeted me on our porch. Cicadas trilled, apathetic to my heartbreak. I dialed Lidia with a measure of shame. Brinn knew me too well. Well enough to gut me.

"Five minutes," Lidia said after my shaky plea for rescue.

It took six.

Her Volkswagen creaked up the driveway, brakes objecting to years of overuse. I let myself sob as I slid into the passenger seat, menthol burning my already bloodshot eyes. Lidia cocked her wrist toward me, offering the breath spray.

"No, thanks," I managed.

There was no further explanation needed as Lidia pulled out of the neighborhood and onto the highway. She'd heard it all before: the mistrust, Brinn's rage at the accusations, round and around and around we'd gone.

My vision was glassy with tears. The wind howled. The cloud dumped buckets of rain like the sky was as shattered as I was.
The Volkswagen pulled left.
A blinding beam of truck lights.
And before the impact, the faintest whiff of tequila.
I'd been alive 28 years.
Had a best friend for 12.
A girlfriend, seven months.

***

"Lidia?" The twinge of fear is laughable. I, a ghost for half a year, nervous about contacting the other side through a Hasbro game. It might've been funny if it weren't so pathetic. "Lidia." I clear my throat. "I contact you from the other—no." I swallow, straighten my back. "Lidia, speak to me."

My hands hover over the planchette, fingers kissing the perimeter. A few uneasy moments pass.

"Lidia, goddammit!"

"You can put the board away."

I don't turn my head, but I see Lidia from the middle of the stairs, leaning against the doorframe. From the dining room, I spot the gash in her head, hair matted and burgundy around the wound. From my spot on the couch, I'm sure she can see the blister on my neck where the seatbelt burned.

The acrid scent of tequila and mint grows stronger as she approaches. Brinn tells me I smell like gasoline. I guess I've grown used to it.

Death has drained Lidia's once warm-toned skin of color. She kneels beside the coffee table, bluish hands folding the board and placing it carefully back in its box. "Well?" She cocks a brow over her mangled eye socket, the remaining eye questioning me in electric blue.

"I'm stuck here." I slump into the couch cushions.

Lidia stacks the games back into their drawer, one by one.

I don't have to ask if it was her with Brinn that night. I already know. It was her and Brinn all those nights.

She laces her fingers together, flips and turns them. Either they crack or I'm so used to hearing the sound, I imagine it.

"So, nothing new then," she says, sitting beside me.

We both stare at the black T.V. screen, surrounded by unread books and dusty tchotchkes.

"Was it... Did you—"

"Love her?"

The words make me salivate with nausea.

"No."

"Did she?"

Lidia picks at a hole in her jeans, where a bit of glass sparkles. "I don't know. I think so."

In the bedroom upstairs, Brinn wakes with a jolt. Sweat has broken out along her hairline, and she throws the covers aside. Lidia must see it too, because her lips draw into a tight line. When Brinn appears on the landing, her cheeks flush pleasant pink, eyes glittering with tears of longing. Another kick in my rotted gut.

I am not the ghost you wanted.

Brinn descends the stairs like a debutante making a wonder-filled society debut. In each step the distance between us closes, and the distance between us grows more clear.

"I should go," Lidia says.

I grab her shoulder. "You can't."

"I can." She shakes me off.

"Lidia, wait, please!" Brinn jogs the remaining steps, steadying herself on the bannister.

Halfway to the door, Lidia pauses. She looks to Brinn who winces at her mutilated face, but tries to hide it in an anxious smile.

"I know," I say, forcing strength into my voice, and both glance in my direction while managing to avoid eye contact. "You wish it was *her*. Stuck here with you."

The air conditioner kicks on, a low hum.

"You wish I'd never made that promise."

Lidia looks at the floor.

Brinn bites her inner lip.

My best friend moves across the hardwood, silent. Her blue eye finds my brown ones. "I have to go." She slides a mournful thumb down my jawline. "I can't save you this time." Lidia thins, now just a stain on the air.

Brinn clasps her palm to her mouth. "No!" is muffled.

"I'm sorry," Lidia says.

And the room is empty but for me and Brinn and the hum of AC.

Brinn chokes back the sob lodged in her throat. "I'm going to bed."

She trudges up the steps, each creaking under her heavy footfalls.

A wild twitch of envy.

Giltiné

Published by Ghost Orchid Press in *Les Petites Morts*, July 2023

Time worn headstones jut up amongst gnarled tree roots in the yellow wood. Four days since I was bitten, the fetid, syrupy smell from my leg wafts from twin boreholes around my ankle. My surrounding skin is a shade of indigo, and spidery veins of deep purple wrap my calf, tendrils extending by the hour. So when I see her, clothed in white, billowing skirts, leaning over a grave to pray, my heart is light with near-forgotten hope. I stagger toward the forgotten cemetery, dragging my rotted leg, and manage to eke out, "Good woman," before my sweat turns cold and I collapse to my knees.

I clutch soft grasses like a lover's hair, and when I glance upward, she looks down upon me. Dappled light cascades through the tree cover, illuminating her soft features.

"Vladas, you look unwell," she says, her tongue wetting her full lips.

"How do you—" My vision is obscured by winking spots, the colors of my wound, and fresh sweat beads on my brow. I let my gaze drop onto a twisted blade of grass. I must have told her my name.

Strong, thin arms roll me to my back. Her ashen hair falls in loose waves and tickles my neck.

"Allow me to take a look," she says, crouching between my parted legs and rolling my pant leg up to the knee. Her pale eyes pass over the bite.

Shame clenches my abdomen as I brace for her to recoil from the smell, but she only *tsks* at me, circling a pointed finger above my mottled flesh.

"It was a—"

"A snake, yes," she says. "I can see as much. And four days it has taken you to find me."

Had I told her this too? I roll through my memory, searching it as a ledger, but I am distracted by firm pressure on my chest. She hovers over me, on palms and knees like a thirsty beast. The scent of rot and death grows stronger, and her fingernails grate my flesh through the fabric of my shirt. My eyes lock on hers, cool colors I can't distinguish. A swirl of mossy green and perhaps the kiss of a lilac wildflower, but then a glimmer of light refracts a golden hue. I find myself entranced by the patterns of it.

Her delicate finger pushes greasy hair from my face, and a warmth from her body—or from within myself—steadies the shiver I had grown used to. She inhales deeply, and my chest expands with hers, a smile exposing her too-white teeth. I gain a sense that—

"It is as if you know me." The words fall from my lips as easily and naturally as an apple from a tree.

"And yet, I am a stranger to you." There's a sorrow in her words, or perhaps a longing.

A gust of wind pushes her shoulder strap down her arm, and the fabric of her dress tumbles with it, exposing the deep plunge between her breasts. She leans forward, close enough to kiss me, but instead whispers into my mouth. "I wish to know you."

The weight of searing pain is lifted, replaced by lust that beats steady as my heart between my thighs. This cannot be. A fever, perhaps. Or a strange dream at the precipice of death.

She draws my shirt over my head, my pants and undergarments down past my ankles. There's no pain from the mortal wound. In fact, I scarcely remember pain. The throbbing lust is too present. I see nothing but her elusive eyes, the goosed skin of her chest, the gentle wave of her hair rolling in the wind.

"Do you wish to know me?"

I'm stark naked, gazing up at her form. My eyes seek to penetrate the opaque linens draping her delicate frame. "I do."

Her expression changes, and there's an unsettling quality I cannot place. She hikes up her skirt, and my blood rushes. I think she might sit upon me, but instead she steps over my broken nakedness. Her bare feet step lightly through young grasses, and she kneels beside a freshly dug grave.

I shrink.

"Who have you come to mourn?" I can think of naught else to say, and I cover myself with my hands, hoping she will not notice the flush of scarlet in my cheeks.

"Mourn?" She doesn't turn, but dips her head into the dirt like the strange cousin of a prayer. Featherlight movement draws my attention to my right shoulder, then my left, and I gasp as hundred-legged insects burrow up from the dirt and crawl across my clavicle.

"Good woman!" There's panic in my voice I can't hide, and as I think my horror cannot grow, a rotund beetle lands atop my cheek, its iridescent wings casting many hues, not unlike her eyes. I swat it away with a fury, abandoning my limp shame to hang unprotected in the fading daylight.

"You do not know me." Her maw is coated in upturned soil, and I think I see a serpentine tongue coil and hide behind her teeth. But it must be the fever. "Four days you have journeyed to find me, and now you have, as my sister has ordained it. And you will know me."

As fear thrums my body and I think to run, she stands once more, slips the dress from her slender form. Her body is flawless as marble, unpainted and freshly carved by a master. I've never seen skin so fair, so wholly unblemished. Svelte legs lead my eyes to the curve of her fruits, and my tongue dries, throat closes; only tasting her will sate my thirst. It's not desire, but a craving I feel, a burning, not from my leg but from the wholeness of my body and soul. I must have her. Must possess her. I want nothing but to drown between her slender thighs.

"And so you shall." Her voice is a cooling breeze. My heart rejoices at her approach, and I've never known true happiness until she plants her feet at each of my cheeks. I gaze upon her loveliness, the curves of her backside.

"Please," is all I can say. She crouches and, in her infinite generosity, gifts me my sole desire. The benevolent goddess presses herself to my lips, and my all too eager mouth opens to accept her.

Her taste is all too sweet! She is fruit of a forbidden wood! Her angle shifts, and I think she might take me into her mouth, but I'm lost in the ecstasy of her swirling across my tongue, sliding down my throat, and I feel a tug at my injured leg. My knee bends, and as I thrust my tongue inside her, delicate fingers wrap around my ankle.

Her lips send shockwaves through my body, but the delicious pressure is not upon my manhood, it's at my ankle, where she sucks—not sucks, but nurses at my necrotic wound.

It must be fever.

It must be a dream.

But the sensation of her mouth upon me while mine swallows her is euphoria I've never known. Surely something otherworldly, surely something divine possesses me. My skin tingles, my very blood vibrates, every muscle and organ radiates pleasure, longing unmatched. Eyes closed, mouth as wide as it will open, I envision myself upon the edge of a roaring fall. White water churns all around me, and the old gods urge me to plunge, to descend to the viscous unknown.

I dive.

Rapturous pleasure rocks my form. Though I have taken many maidens, I am virginal to this most sublime reckoning. My eyes crack open through wave after wave of ecstasy, and once again she hovers above me, her pale skin now shot through with deep purple tendrils. They stretch, twist, and expand, covering her form in midnight death.

Eik su manimi. A voice not my own beckons me to come, and she faces me on her palms and knees, her irises darkening to a cloudless, nebula sky. When her lips touch mine, the fetid, syrupy scent fills my nostrils. A serpentine tongue reaches into my throat. My thoughts clear. And I understand.

"Giltiné," I say, choked, as my flesh takes on the color of her eyes. "Mirties Deivė, Goddess of Death."

There's a glimmer in her inky eyes. "Alas, you know me."

It's the last thing I hear, a cold comfort as my body descends into the earth. Soft dirt envelopes me like a deep pool, many-legged insects pull me down like the rush of roaring water, the ever-growing weight of the living world sits atop my chest, the crushing pressure of a deep sea.

And then nothing.

Between Her Teeth

Through the jungle and into the mountains, Kong carried me, fragments of rope still dangling from my wrists. Warm liquid rolled down my face, a cocktail of rain and bits of Ralph tumbling from the beast's hairy jaw. Ralph's screams echoed in my mind, made me feel faint. The sound of bone crunching through the beast's canines, the muffled gasp, the agony's abrupt stop, that final slurp. And my husband-to-be was gone.

Perhaps the humidity was going to my head, perhaps the trauma was simply too much for any woman to bear, but Kong's footsteps–steady and strong through the dense undergrowth–lulled me into a strange sense of calm. I can't say how long he marched upward, only that fog rolled in, then out again, that the stars had slightly shifted position and the clouds had swallowed the moon, when we finally reached the rocky outcropping. Above the treeline, whispers of smoke painted the air, a final reminder of the village that offered me up.

The fight and ensuing journey must've tired the ape, for he jostled me with huffing breaths. Dizzy as I was, it was a relief when he set me down on a narrow ledge. Knees quaking, I braced myself to stand, eyes trained on the dusty floor.

A guttural grunt commanded I face him.

Watery blood ran between the cracks in my lips, shocking me with a taste of iron. He extended what I could only describe as a torso-sized pointer finger. I thought surely the time had come, the march had hungered the beast once more, and he would scoop me up and chew my sinew just as he had Ralph's, but instead, with remarkable gentleness, Kong nudged my chin upward with his gargantuan fingertip.

Dark eyes, impossibly large, fixed on me. The lines of his face smoothed. No longer did his jowls pull back into an angry snarl. Rather than a twist of fury in his brow, I saw curiosity—dare I say, concern. A sliver of the moon, released from its prison of clouds, reflected in the beast's iris. And as I gazed deeply inside, I thought I saw, for the first time, that face so often spoken of as *the man in the moon*. Except, it was not a man.

It was the slender face of a woman. So much like my own.

His pupils shifted, causing me to turn. I shrieked at what I found. Within the rocky outcropping, something I hadn't seen before, an opening, an entrance, a cave, and emerging from it, another woman, then another behind her. A third woman emerged, and they stood in a line. They shared my fear, but it was not the beast that made them pale: it was me. Tentatively, they took in my appearance, and it was then I straightened my dress—as best I could, anyway, the thin strap having been torn, the silk stained with hair and sweat and blood.

I blinked the tears from my eyes, images of the women becoming clear.

"Fay?"

The first nodded, her auburn hair dingy with oil but unmistakable, even in the low light. She turned to the others, "Jessica," she said, pointing at the first.

"And Naomi." I'd heard so much talk of her emerald eyes, men lamenting the loss of the handsome children she might have bore them.

Naomi nodded.

"You're alive?"

A tiny smile carved a fissure in Fay's cheek. "So it would seem."

"And you've been here…"

"All this time," she finished, seeming to speak for the others, stepping slightly forward, extending her palm to make my acquaintance.

"Esther," I offered. "In town, they…" I would've liked to tell the women they were mourned, that tales were spun of their brave sacrifice, but in truth, the only whispers were of beauty wasted, sentiments of *better her than us*. She gave me a dainty but confident shake, sparing me from finishing the thought.

Kong grunted as if pleased, then took lumbering steps around the corner, disappearing behind rock and tree, hiding his massive form as if by some unknown magic. Unseen footsteps rumbled the earth as it moved away, then turned to low vibrations before vanishing entirely. A cool wind goosed my flesh, and I didn't know whether to be relieved that the thing was gone, or to fear these wild women, haggard from rough living, whose means of survival and motives remained a mystery.

Questions rose and stuck in my throat before I could utter a word, but Fay spoke first, sparing me the trial of discerning which was most appropriate to ask.

"Come inside."

Naomi led the way into the cave, followed dutifully by Jessica. Fay hesitated at the entrance, and I surmised from her pause that she wished me to enter before her. The stone was cold but smooth beneath my bare feet, and it seemed my guess was correct, as the moment I crossed the threshold, Fay closed the space behind me.

Claustrophobia wrapped tendrils around my chest. Walls pressed in on all sides, the ceiling short enough I had to stoop, moist rock encompassing me on either side, Jessica just steps ahead and Fay blocking the path behind. Pale moonlight faded to nothing as we traversed the slim passage, and I was once again swallowed by inky darkness. My breaths came short and ragged. We walked on. Walls seemed to bend inward as if reaching for me. The path seemed to grow colder, siphoning heat from the soles of my feet. My thoughts swirled, and just as I thought I might faint from the sensation of being consumed by rock and blackness, a warm glow slithered its way from the space ahead. The stony walls expanded, like the mountain itself had taken a great inhale. Fay's hand pressed the small of my back, urging me onward until the cave opened up into something like a room, the warm stomach of the mountain. Fire crackled in the center, and at the outer corners lay three, makeshift beds. I say beds, for I understood this must be their intended use; but in all actuality, they were little more than a collection of shredded palm fronds draped in stained fabric.

"Sit," Fay said.

It was only then I noticed that Jessica and Naomi were not merely quiet, they regarded me with skepticism, unease. And while I took for granted that the three beds were distributed one to each of them, I reconsidered when Jessica and Naomi sat next to one another on the same, oversized frond, drawing a shared, frazzled bit of fabric over both their pairs of legs.

"It's lucky you're here," Fay said, and I couldn't help but laugh.

Lucky? Lucky my fiance had been torn to bits by this thing? Lucky I'd been chosen as tribute at all? My face must have betrayed my shock, for she went on.

"Why were you chosen?" she asked, though she must know, having been selected herself some years prior, no doubt based on the very same criteria.

"They need—" My voice cracked, a sudden soreness in my throat, no doubt from all my screaming some hours before. "A virginal tribute, as I'm sure you remember."

"Right." She tucked a strand of hair behind her ear, reaching both palms toward the crackling flames to warm herself. "And are you?"

I followed suit, scooting toward the fire on my rump, hoping the flames would chase away the encroaching chill, while knowing the damp walls were only partially responsible for it. I once again thought of Ralph, his clumsy kisses, his grasping hands, and how I'd fended off his advances time and time again: at the theater, on those tense walks home, within the confines of his motor car. And the time I could not.

"Well?" Fay pressed.

Naomi busied herself, combing through the tangles in Jessica's hair. It felt like a tremendous burden to tear my eyes from the way Jessica's eased shut, seemingly in pleasure at the sensation.

My shame was no business of hers, so I said, "Yes," heat rushing to my cheeks as I spied Naomi's hand drift luridly close to the underside of Jessica's breast.

A rustling of sticks alerted me to Fay's movement, and when I glanced up at her, she'd moved to my side, letting her heel graze my calf as she settled.

"Why would you say that?" I blurted.

"Say what?" Fay replied, fixing her stare upon me with an intensity that froze me like prey, though—I admit—it was not altogether unwelcome.

"That I was lucky."

"Did you relish the life that was waiting for you?" Fay's breath landed neatly on my shoulder, and a bead of sweat rolled down my collarbone. The cave's belly had not only warmed my chill, the heat inside was near stifling.

"I was to be married." The croak over the last word was, in part, due to the hoarseness of my throat, but the idea of my pending nuptials had often been the source of discomfort, an uncomfortable choke even before I'd been chosen for the beast.

Hair lifted off my neck, twisted into a bun in Fay's palm. "You're safe from that now." And suddenly I felt the mad suspicion that she'd been privy to my most private thoughts. "Our queen has a way of choosing," she went on, carefully unweaving the shredded rope at each of my wrists before encircling my midsection.

"What do you mean?" Color flooded my cheeks. I told myself it was indignation. "Ralph died defending me."

"Defending *you*?" The words lashed like a whip. "Or his property?"

"I…" came out as a whisper.

"Surely, you must know the difference." She pulled me in tighter, my body rigid in her hold. "Do you want me to stop?" she breathed into my ear.

I said nothing, could say nothing! But mercifully, Fay released me and relaxed into a posture more befitting a lady. A flick of her hand led me to look back at Jessica and Naomi, and my heart all but stopped beating when I found them locked in a sensuous kiss, Jessica's hands running wild across Naomi's body.

"As I said," Fay went on, undaunted, "our queen selects us quite carefully."

"You—" I stammered.

"Are you not?"

I was, once again, invaded. "What *queen*? What are you implying?" I pushed myself a few more inches away from her.

"In town, they call her King. But they are wrong, as they are about so many things. She is and ever has been a queen."

I thought back to the hairy beast, fangs the size of tree trunks glistening with viscera.

"She is unlike them, so they fear her. But you are unlike them too. Are you not?" Fay lowered her voice to a whisper. "More like Naomi and Jessica. And me."

By this point Naomi had climbed atop Jessica's body, pressing into her with undulating movements, Jessica's moans stifled only by the closeness of their mouths.

"They would fear you too." Fay leaned back on her arms, the curves of her body illuminated by the firelight. "If they knew."

I shook my head, lost for words. But found I could not separate my eyes or my mind from the throes of passion happening just feet away.

"She knew by your smell. She's never wrong."

Slickness bled between my thighs, a hollow craving more savage than hunger taking up residence in my core. "Is that why she didn't…"

"Eat you?" Fay said it so matter-of-factly, I might have thought we were discussing the weather. She didn't wait for me to answer before confirming. "The hateful find violence between her teeth, but we've found—"

Jessica cried out, a passionate shriek that caused a twitch in my most sensitive places. It echoed off the damp cave walls, seemed to reverberate again and again, sound bouncing and distorting until it took on the cadence of drums. Steady drums. But no, the pitch was wrong, and instead of the sound fading and dying away, it grew louder. Not drums, not echoes, but footsteps drawing close.

"It's time," Fay said, standing. Unceremoniously, she pulled me to my feet, gesturing toward the path from where we'd come. She laced her fingers in mine as Jessica watched, panting from her makeshift bed, Naomi smoothing perspiration from her face. Neither made a move to follow.

"Don't fight her," Fay said as we walked, once again consumed by darkness as the firelight faded to nothing and the cave walls pressed in close. "Trust me. Trust her."

The sound of my feet on stone blended with the hammering in my chest. Something edging on fear with all the electricity of titillation drove me onward. Again I felt

Fay had wormed her way into my private spaces. I felt seen, studied, discovered, but for the first time, not alone. I gripped Fay's hand, and when we reached the mouth of the cave, the beast was waiting, a flicker of lust in her vast, dark eyes.

"Do as I do," Fay said, stepping to the edge of the outcropping. Kong extended her palm, and Fay stepped into it without hesitation. She raised Fay into the air, Fay crouching to keep her balance. The beast pressed Fay's body to her cheek, drawing a long inhale of her scent, lids fluttering much like Jessica's had at Naomi's gentle touch.

I stood transfixed as Fay ran her hand along Kong's mighty lips. When they parted slightly, Fay sat upon the bottom lip as she might a fine couch, rubbing her hands back and forth on either side of her as if appreciating an imported fabric.

To my shock and horror, the ache between my legs only grew. I shifted my weight, fighting the urge to reach beneath the shreds of my dress. Despite the violence I'd only just witnessed, I longed to see those mighty canines once more, to see the moisture of the jungle king's—no, queen's—tongue coat Fay's body in a viscous sheen.

I know not whether Fay or my new queen heard my secret desire, but my wish was granted when, in a fluid motion, a tongue wrapped Fay entirely and drew her between the jutting teeth, into the dark and cavernous mouth. Compelled forward, I stepped to the ledge, and just as she had for Fay, Kong extended a flat palm, which I stepped onto. Having seen the swiftness of her movement with Fay, I straddled one of the great fingers, wrapping my arms around the knuckle for purchase. The pressure against my center offered a pleasant bit of relief to the urgent craving inside, and gingerly, she drew me to her nose, taking a great whiff that sent shivers across my back. Her lips were plump and smooth, and I too found myself running my palms along them, feeling the bit of moisture on the inner corners.

Like a woman possessed, I gave in completely to my need, swinging one leg over her bottom lip and wrapping my body around the pillowy form. A groan rattled her mammoth chest, sending vibrations that very nearly led me to shatter, but stopped just short of it. Deranged with desire, I writhed against her, the smooth flesh offering just enough resistance to build my lust to a frenzy. I worked my body against her as I'd seen Naomi do to Jessica, longing for the same result, the Earth-shattering scream that shook the mountain and summoned Kong back to us, but before I could reach my precipice, her tongue, dripping with saliva, scooped me inside with both the force of a hurricane and the care of a lover.

Total darkness.

The only sound was Kong's thumping pulse and the occasional swallow which sucked me tight to her inner cheek. There, I found Fay, naked—or rather, she found me. Slender fingers crept to the crest of my thighs, and I cried out in ecstasy, no longer constrained by the fears or beliefs of men and the outside world. I let Fay's tongue enter my mouth, the silken lining of Kong's cheeks a pulsing blanket on all sides. What I wanted was madness. Yet still, I wanted so strongly.

To be inhabited.

Filled.

Devoured.

Fay teased my opening, rubbing my slit and stopping just short of piercing me when she whispered in my ear, "Do you want me to show you true pleasure?"

"Yes!" The answer came in a long, agonizing groan. And with that, Fay's arms came to my hips, throwing me along with herself into the queen's yawning throat.

All constricted.

A tight pressure wracked my body and I lost all sense of up or down, pushed through tissue by rhythmic movement. The heat was like an expertly drawn tub, hot enough to relax, but not enough to burn. Fay's body tangled with mine as we moved through this most unknown, secret space, and when we landed somewhere soft and slick.

Her stomach.

Tingling alerted me to the dangerous reality: I'd been swallowed, consumed, now submerged in digestive acid. Was I trapped? How easily could Kong simply meander back into the jungle, forget her affection for Fay and me, and let us slowly succumb?

Trust me. Trust her. I heard the words again as Fay smoothed errant hairs from my neck. The gesture stirred my lust, and I let myself collapse as Fay tore my panties and spread my legs, planting my knees on her shoulders and letting her tongue slide through my center in confident strokes. I shimmied my dress over my head, it was little more than tatters by this point anyway. Every bit of my flesh met warmth, slickness, satiny, hungry, living need. The very walls expanded and contracted, pushing and pulling. I felt suction unlike anything I'd ever experienced, one that drew all heat, all consciousness to the apex of my thighs. Clenching my fingertips into the tissue surrounding me, Kong released a grumble of pleasure. Her groan shook the belly of the beast, sending another set of vibrations through Fay's tongue and into me, and all the screaming desire I'd stowed away came crashing through me in a riptide of pleasure that stopped time and left me panting, disoriented, and utterly sated.

I'd scarcely collected my thoughts when a torrent of pressure threw me from my decadent bed. Rocketing forth at a dizzying speed, I didn't have time to be afraid, for when I cracked open my eyes, I was back on the rocky outcropping, Fay by my side, drenched head to toe, as I was, in yellow-tinged fluids.

A smirk cracked Fay's lips.

Kong pushed red-speckled slime from my nose and mouth, a gesture that made me nuzzle into her touch. Fay fished the remains of my dress from a nearby pool of goo, wrung it out and slid it over my frame. "You did well," she whispered, then lowered herself into a bow, saliva dripping from her crown. Surrounding us lay chunks of what appeared to be slimy meat. "My queen," she said, catching her breath from the recent exertion.

Fay held the position until I realized I should do the same, stumbling to my feet and dropping my head in an awkward curtsey. "My queen."

A beat passed, and when I glanced up, Kong bore an unmistakable look of satisfaction before turning and disappearing once more into the trees.

Fay straightened and took to gathering chunks of masticated flesh. Horror raised the fine hairs on the back of my neck.

"Is that…" I stopped myself, because it could only be one thing, dwelling beside us in Kong's belly while I reached the height of my rapture, and now thrown forth from that same belly—

Ralph.

"What else do you expect us to eat?"

I felt a wave of revulsion, but Fay, arms heavy with raw hunks of muscle, slipped into the cave's entrance, and what could I do but follow?

"Aren't you hungry?" she called back to me in the dark.

A grumble told me I was. I was hungry. I thought once more about Ralph's grasping hands as Fay and I thrust deeper into the mountain, til firelight broke through the blackness once more, and we were greeted by Jessica and Naomi, who'd set up a roasting spit in our absence.

Fay handed Naomi a mound of flesh, and Jessica retrieved a meat cleaver from their shared bed space.

"I'm starved."

A Fine Wife, Indeed

From the moment I met her cobblestone eyes, I knew I would possess her, this woman of the sea. She must love me, for daily she arrives with the breaking of dawn, languishing about the mossy boulders, tossing her ashen hair. I could pick out the interwoven bits of kelp. How fine she would look in emerald silks! On the third morning, fishermen long set out to their work and the shoreline clear of all but we two, she speaks to me.

"Come," she says, with a sweeping motion of her hand. Between the fingers, translucent webbing froths the tide. Easily, I could trim it away, slide a golden band in its place. "Lifetimes, I have waited for you."

"Tell me your name." Though I've never heard of one in the tales, even a seal woman should have a name.

"Alysandra," she says, her voice like a hiss.

Alysandra Clark. It has a ring to it.

"You've a broad chest, sir. Strong arms. Surely, you must swim." Again, she beckons me forward; and—as if on her command—the pebbles beneath me shift, and I catch myself to keep from stumbling into the tidepool.

I consider her invitation, eyes wandering over dark clouds on the horizon. Flashes of light lacerate the sky, and while I long to slip off my boots and trousers, to join her in the shallows, to warm her flesh with my own, it would be a fool's errand. "A storm approaches," I say. "But I would host you in my home, should you care to join me on land."

Her chin dips below the waterline, reflection of the water's surface distorting her grin. "Sir—" The word twists over a barrage of bubbles. "—You know that I cannot."

"But you can." I step forward and crouch, ignoring the seepage of water into my socks. "Until midnight, as the tales go. Or is that mere story and song?"

At this, the smile reaches her eyes. She draws herself up to her full height, water pouring off her naked form, nipples perked from the kiss of air. Her hips are wide enough to bear many sons. I extend my hand and she accepts it, stepping easily through the broken shells and slickness of the shoreline. When both her feet are firmly planted, I shift, sliding my jacket from one shoulder, then the next, placing it around her.

"Does my body bring you shame?" She makes no move to draw it around her bare breasts. Her sex is hidden only by pale hair, glistening with beaded water.

I make a cursory show of averting my eyes, but a throb between my legs beckons me to take her here and now, to lay her down, watch her squirm when the unforgiving shore steals strips of flesh from her back, thrust into her, fill her with me and my legacy.

"Sir?"

"No." I hope she pays no mind to the quick flick of my head. "My cottage is just over the hill." I indicate a circle of trees crowned with morning fog.

"Your cottage?"

"Aye." She matches my quickened pace, and a roll of thunder echoes off the ocean behind us. "Many years it has belonged to my family."

The farther we draw from the beach, the more frantically I cast looks behind me, hoping she might eye the spot where she's hidden her skin. I cannot let her disappear beneath the surf, not after waiting these long years for my perfect bride. And to think, she awaited me too, in my hometown, all this time! I look again. But her stony gaze betrays nothing.

"You've not told me your name," she says, now just an acre from the cottage.

"Edwin."

"Edwin Clark," she repeats, as if rolling the sound over her tongue.

Had I told her my surname? I must have.

Our family goat bleats a welcome as we reach the trodden path to our front door. Alysandra's chin tilts to follow the flash of movement behind our sheer curtain. "With whom do you share your home?"

"Just my grandmother." In my mind, I curse her presence. She should be well on her way to town by now. I suppose she's not even yet gathered the eggs for market. "Pay her no mind."

Alysandra's expression twists in a way I cannot recognize.

"Are you hungry?" I swing the door open wide, salt-crusted brass groaning at the hinge.

A shrug.

Grandmother turns, dropping a tray of biscuits, sending crumbs skittering across the floor. Out of womanly instinct, Alysandra stoops over and gathers the bits near her. She will make a fine wife, indeed.

"Apologies! My clumsy hands." Grandmother chirps, fumbling about to toss biscuits back into their tray. It's then she fixes her gaze on Alysandra, and time seems to stop for her too, as it did for me when I recognized my bride.

"Grandmother, this is Alysandra."

Grandmother's jaw hangs open, browned teeth exposed. Between the frazzled locks of silver hair, I spot a dumbfounded expression, and think for a moment the old woman might have finally parted ways with her senses. Alysandra, too, must think it, for she freezes in place, as if waiting to be attacked by some feral beast.

I move to usher Grandmother out of the room when she speaks. "Alysandra—" A cough. "—it is lovely to meet you."

"Likewise." My bride assumes a dreamy look, reaching toward Grandmother with all the hesitation of a child capturing a dragonfly.

"Minerva." Grandmother takes Alysandra's hand, but not in greeting. I wince with embarrassment as Grandmother laces her fingers through my bride's, recoiling slightly when her twisted knuckles meet the webbing.

"My grandmother was just leaving," I offer, and finally the gods smile on me, for she takes my meaning, placing the remaining biscuits on the tray, and shuffling out the backdoor.

Alysandra turns up her nose, no doubt flustered at the old woman's cloddishness.

"Sorry about her," I mutter. "Let us get you some clothes."

She allows me to lead her into grandmother's room, where I cast open the closet and blow a sheen of dust from the wardrobe of her youth. Flipping through, I locate a camise, white satin, befitting a bride with little mind for modesty, and pass it to Alysandra.

"You would like me to cover myself?"

Her strangeness tests my patience. "I should like you to make yourself decent."

A relenting nod is a positive sign. She is open to learning. Tossing my jacket from her shoulders, she steps into the camise, slipping her arms through the straps.

"A vision," I say, her curves even more lovely when partially obscured by the thin fabric.

"Do you love me, Edwin Clark?" It comes out flat, no hint as to her preference for my answer.

"I mean to make you my bride."

Alysandra sits upon the floral bedspread, and I'm suddenly aware of the scent of aging. It wafts from the fabric, cotton knitted by aching hands.

"A daytime bride?" she asks, palm running over the pale pink roses. "It was my impression that men prefer their wives in the nighttime hours."

I cannot contain my laugh. "A bride at all hours."

"And yet you know, I must return to my home come midnight, lest I die here. Surely, you want a living bride and not a corpse?"

A sinking feeling. "I'd hoped…" I pace a tight circle. "We might save this discussion for this evening, but since you've asked, I've a plan in mind. Should you gift me your skin, you may stay with me on land. Isn't that right?"

She chuckles, worrying at a stitched yellow circle of pollen. "It is not mine to give. You must come into the water, ask my father for my hand. If he deems you worthy, he may gift it to you. But if not…" She trails off, rudely.

I take a deep breath. It's unrealistic to expect she would understand manners, but she will come to learn.

"A bit of a predicament then." I tire of her distractedness, raising her chin to face me. "For I would drown, should I go plodding into the sea."

"How unfortunate." She stands and steps toward the door without even a glance in my direction.

I grab her shoulder. "Wait." It's then I think of the secret thing, long buried.

"There's no sense in delaying the inevitable," she says, facing me with shallow disappointment. "You'll need to find another bride."

Though I was sworn to secrecy, I cannot let my chance at a happy marriage escape me. "There is a way." I clasp her by the elbow, leading her through the cottage and backdoor. Grandmother is nowhere to be seen, likely well on her way to market by now, so I lead Alysandra to the great oak, where Grandfather carved his initials, where he spoke in hushed tones.

It's warm, the morning sun having burned up most of the fog, but I take the shovel from the creaky wheelbarrow, crack the grass with its lip, and start digging. Alysandra makes herself comfortable at the base of the tree, intermittently asking, *Shall I fetch you some water? Might I help in some way?*

She will make a fine wife, indeed.

Half an hour's passed when the lip of my shovel meets unusual resistance. I pry the thing upward, tight hide, baked in an oven of soil and heat and time. I think I spy a bit of wetness in Alysandra's eyes, perhaps the shade did not shelter her from the heat as much as I thought it might. Yanking the thing from the earth, I present it to her, chest swelled.

"With this, I can meet your father, request your hand."

"Aye." Her voice cracks.

"Let's get you back inside." I encircle her in my arm, dragging the rotted thing behind us. "I'll not have my bride succumb to heat stroke before we take our vows."

***

Alysandra is sat by the window, sipping a frosty glass I fetched from the icebox, condensation rolling to her wrist, when I ask, "It will work, will it not?"

I hold the stinking hide to my chest, trying and failing to imagine my transformation into a blubbery creature.

"So say the legends and songs." Her mind is elsewhere, gaze fixed on the split between the curtains. Does she wait for some other husband to rescue her? Or perhaps she just longs for the sea.

"Do not be coy."

A sharp look. "It will work."

I lift the glass from her, placing it on the counter beside the soiled biscuits. "Well then." I gesture at the door.

Alysandra follows me—in a manner of speaking—but does such with insect-like patterns, bobbing and weaving, taking languid, lazy steps. I have to circle back twice to keep from gaining too much distance. Storm clouds have advanced from the north, dimming the sea with an inky cast. I'm remiss to think of plunging into the churning waters in this weather, but I'll not let my chance slip away as a result of my own trepidation.

She's running her hands through a patch of grasses when I reach the rocky shoreline, and I have to bite at my cheek to keep from reprimanding her for moving so idly.

"Alysandra!" I drape the seal hide over my neck. "Come!" With the word, lightning splits the sky in half, rain speckling her face.

She turns toward it, outstretching her arms, letting the patter soak the white satin.

"Alysandra!"

Instead of heeding me, she spins, slowly, parting her lips to welcome the storm into her mouth. I hope she will welcome me as eagerly. The camise turns translucent, and I fight that same urge to rip it from her body, to take her upon the seagrass, no matter how it slices her flesh.

But I must be patient, have already waited this long, and we are so close, indeed.

"Alysandra, now!" This gets her attention, and as another roll of thunder bounces off the tumbling waves, she jogs up to join me at the shoreline.

"Finally." I say it under my breath, but loud enough for her to hear. Pressing the hide to my back, then my chest, I give her a look. Why isn't it working?

She steps into the tidepool from whence she came. "You must come into the water."

Begrudgingly, I kick off my boots. Jagged shells scratch the soles of my feet through my socks, but I press forward, following my bride into the shallows, where thankfully, the sand grows finer, the rocks more sparse.

As if a seam's been ripped in the sky, the patter of rain turns torrential, silver sheets obscuring the view more than a few feet, but Alysandra's attention turns to a high place on the jetty. I squint against the storm, water pouring off my brows, and make out a plump, hunched figure.

Grandmother.

"Go home," I scream against the tempest. But either she doesn't hear me, or pays me no mind.

"Come deeper," Alysandra says, sinking down so she's submerged to the shoulders.

The hide is unwieldy, dragging against my efforts, but I follow, fighting the churning tide.

With a plop, Alysandra disappears beneath the surface, and I glance back toward Grandmother, finding she's no longer perched on the jetty.

I dunk, flailing my arms to find Alysandra, to demand she tell me how the magic works, so I might transform, move as nimbly as she in the water. But the sea is churned. Sand and kelp are all I find beneath the waves, and when I resurface, there's a crack at the back of my head.

I catch myself on a nearby boulder, vision tipping and blurring. Rainwater runs into my eyes—not rainwater, blood.

Splashing nearby grabs my attention.

Grandmother, sloshing into the sea. I reach toward her, but her gaze is elsewhere. Nausea threatens to spill bile from my belly, but I refocus, find Alysandra has emerged from the white caps.

I yell, my attempt at her name coming out as little more than a gargle.

Beside me floats the rotted hide, but it's snatched up…by a wave? The world tips over and rights itself. I lose my footing but find it again. Not a wave—snatched up by a gnarled hand, twisted knuckles, by Grandmother.

"Gran—" I wretch, spewing hot mess down my chin. Swiping at the warmth running into my eyes, my hand comes away red. A chunk of flesh, hair still clinging to it, slides off my palm and is gobbled up by the current. Black curtains surround my line of vision, but I watch as Grandmother reaches for Alysandra, as Alysandra reaches back, as she welcomes Grandmother into her arms like she did the rain.

Muddled words. Words I can barely discern, but in the shape of, *How I've missed you. How I've longed to hold you. My life. My ocean. My love.*

I've a flash of Grandfather, when he showed me his initials, when he told me of the hide, when he swore me to secrecy.

Lightning strobes the image of Alysandra, or is she wracked with sobs?

Grandmother drapes the hide across her back. My bride holds it there—But perhaps, not my bride? The curtain threatens to close, the world cast in a haze.

Perhaps, never my bride.

Raindrops cascade down the women's faces. Raindrops, or tears.

The air is heavy with longing, or the storm, or the weight of the truth as they both turn: Grandmother, from a haggard old woman to an ageless, plump seal, and Alysandra, from a rare beauty to a creature who never wanted me.

But perhaps, wanted Grandmother.

Perhaps had her, before Grandfather brought her home, thought she would make a fine wife, indeed.

There's a baying and a bark. It's the last thing I hear before the curtain closes, before the sea swallows my body. And between the chittering of sand against rock, of distant, rolling thunder, and barking, baying seals, I glean one last truth: Each, a fine wife. Their marriage baked in dirt, and heat, and churning ocean, and unfeeling men, and uncaring time.

A wife not meant for Grandfather.

A wife not meant for me.

traces of tiny footmarks gobbled up by the ground. Black curtains surround my line of vision, but I watch as Grandmother reaches for Alexantra, as Abysoda reaches back, as the wretches Grandmother into her arms as she did the rain.

'Muddled Words. Words I can hardly discern, but only the shape of. Ahoseeva missed you. Miss I've felt you to don't tou. Ma. Ibe Alexantra. Un deso'.

I've a flash of Grandfather, when he showed me his initials when he told me of the time when he swore me to silence.

I fight the urge to flee instead of Alexsanding or I, she looked with solid.

Grandmother draws the lady across her back. My bride holds it there, but perhaps her my bridge. The curtain threatens to close the world out of her face.

Perhaps never my bride.

Raindrops cascade down this woman's face. Raindrops or tears.

The air is heavy with longing, or the storm, or the weight of the truth as they both turn Grandmother from a haggard old woman to an ancient, plump local. And Alexantra from a mad beauty to a creature whosoever wanted me.

But perhaps wants Grandmother.

'Perhaps', said her, before Grandmother brought her home, though she would make a fine wife, aho?'

'There's a boiling, and a bank. It's the last thing I hear before the curtain closes, before the sea swallows my body. And before the clittering of sand against a rock of distant colling thunder, and darking beyond myself, I grasp one last truth. Back, a fine one. The grimacipi, liked in dying sea beta, and chimming up and unfeelings son, and unseeing time.

A wife not meant for me, mamifiri.

I Gave My Heart to a Hurricane

My parents introduced me to Ian. I'd been feigning interest in my mother's crop of tomatoes, my father's latest bass fishing competition. The TV mumbled from another room, and I might've missed him, had the dog not run off with mom's gardening glove. I chased Chester into the living room where he dropped the glove and skittered beneath a coffee table. It was then, looking up, glove in hand, that I found my soulmate.

The shot centered a store with windows shattered. Palm trees swayed in the background while the reporter groaned about property damage, loss of life. But all around him was Ian: his dark, heavy clouds, his powerful gusts. He sprinkled lightning to catch my eye.

I knew it.

I knew it then, that it was me he came for.

"May I use the computer?"

I didn't wait for an answer. I threw myself into internet searches, printed page after page of spaghetti models. As I ran my finger along their sweet curves, a shiver sent chills creeping across my shoulders.

You are mine. You are mine.

When mom started to balk and dad looked at me queerly, I raced home, printed pages clutched to my chest. I held them close the whole drive, like an ex's hoodie, still smelling of him–not quite him, but the memory, the essence of him.

Ian was with me already.

Days, I had to wait. Days! While others swarmed the gas station, the grocery, the liquor store, I watched him move. Quick and graceful like a panther, he swept through the Caribbean. He tore roofs from homes, flipped vehicles, all looking for me.

I tried to tell him, "I'm here! Keep coming, I'm right here, waiting!" My breath left fog on the TV screen. He must've heard me. He must've. Because steadily, he came.

24 hours out, I tried to schedule with every salon in town. Ringing, and ringing, and ringing. The few who answered did so with furtive confusion, some with horror in their voice when I tried to book. *A state of emergency,* they said. *We have families too.*

I had to settle, ultimately, for a flat iron and YouTube tutorials. Ian deserved my best. I uncovered my most expensive lipstick, the one from my wedding all those years back, and dressed my lips in Black Cherry Winter. Anyone looking at my room would've thought he'd already passed through, clothes strewn about the bed, the chair, the dresser. I tried on everything. Every pair of shoes. Every possible combination. I changed and changed until sweat threatened the edges of my foundation.

It was the sundress I went with, cream colored with bright red roses. He couldn't miss me in this. I paired it with a yellow patent-leather wedge heel.

Streets were empty. I flew east, pushing 90, not a single cop in sight. All the universe conspired to bring us together. The rain was a faint mist, and when I arrived at the beach, the last of the daredevil surfers were fixing their boards to their roof racks. One tried to call after me,

"Hey. HEY!"

But I wouldn't be stopped now. I stumbled a bit, carrying the basket and the blanket and the wine glasses and all. I should've brought my wagon. But in my haste to see him, I'd lost all common sense and left it in the garage.

I'd had a fleeting, unhinged thought to invite my parents. But they wouldn't understand, not after all they'd heard about his history. They'd think I was nuts! And this was between us. Our first meeting, after so much longing.

Long distance relationships are hard. Everyone knows that.

I anchored two points of the blanket with my shoes, one with the wine bottle, and sat on the last. It was no small task, with the wind blowing as it was. He waited until I laid down to make his first move. The gentlest caress sent my skirt billowing upward, and I caught it, feeling very Marilyn Monroe.

"Oh, Ian."

He answered in a croon, a long howling gust that sounded like, *You came*.

"Of course, I came. I've been… I'm just so happy you're here."

A crack of thunder. He felt the same. And though I had to squint against the sand which lashed my face like tiny bullets, I made out his looming figure, a black swell over the churning Atlantic.

"I can't believe you traveled so far, just to see me."

Rain came in sideways droves, turning my sundress translucent. *I want to see more of you.*

And how could I resist? I slipped the dress over my shoulders, let his wind lick at my nipples, making them hard.

He teased me this way until–

"Oh stop, stop!" I said, but he knew from my crooked smile and the glint in my eyes that I wanted more.

I'll give it to you, he said with a tumble of sound. And no sooner had the words reached my ears than a flash exploded from his center and spread across the sky like an atom bomb. The ache between my legs became impossible to ignore, so I shed the rest of my sopping clothes, stood naked on the blanket. Ian had taken my shoes, so it wrapped around my calves, holding me in place.

"You're into the kinky stuff?"

Somewhere in the distance an alarm blared. I turned my cheek to track the noise, but Ian, impatient for me, turned it back. He pushed me toward the sea. With legs tangled in the blanket, I stumbled, landing on all fours in the cool sand. My hands sank to the wrist, but Ian pressed me forward, so I crawled. Buried shells carved divots in my knees. An errant branch whipped past my ear, leaving a scratch on my shoulder which stung in the salty air. But still I pressed on.

"I'm coming!" I screamed it against the wind. Ian swallowed the sound. He was hungry, so hungry for me. When I reached the shoreline, the tide pulsed in and out. There, I struggled to my feet.

"Ian, I'm here! I'm ready for you!"

While his wind tickled my breasts and the onslaught of his rain kissed between my legs, he penetrated me. Not where I expected, to be sure, but Ian was a creative lover. It was massive, five feet! Cold, hard metal thrust hard and deep into my sternum. From the latch, I knew it to be an umbrella, but was only sure when I felt the pull. The delicious pull! It shuddered inside me, a gentle rocking back and forth, back and forth. And then he *really* gave it to me. I heard the crack as the umbrella shot open, then my ears were full of *him*. The pressure was so strong, I faintly felt my feet lift from the ground.

I squeezed my eyes shut to feel him moving inside me, the ache twisting into a pleasurable knot between my legs. But I did sneak one peek. Beneath, a flurry of white water and black sky. I tumbled head over feet as he pulled me close. His pace quickened, my moans swallowed by the sound of waves cresting and collapsing on themselves.

Ian pressed in from all sides, his mouth at my most sensitive places, his voice ringing in my head, his toy beating a rhythm in my chest. So steady, so steady, I shattered, releasing my pleasure in a guttural scream.

With that, he withdrew. As quickly as he grabbed me, he let me go. Hair flew upward as I raced down, and Ian snatched his pole, left a gaping emptiness in its wake.

I gave you my heart.

It was the last thought I had before crashing into the swirling sea.

Eyes Open, Knees Apart for the End of the World

Published by Hungry Shadow Press in The First Five Minutes of the Apocalypse, August 2023

Sarah was about to come when the apocalypse started.

Her abdomen clenched, mind finally free of unfolded laundry, the tone of that PR woman's email, the ingrown hair festering in her upper thigh. Her free hand gripped the blankets and her back raised from the mattress in a serpentine arch. Above the buzzing, one phrase echoed over and over in her mind: *You like that you dirty little—*

Then the shadow of a boom. The first, they'd been told, in a series of explosions. Ringing bounced off every wall and the tile floor, or did it emanate from inside her own head? And just as the dust cloud rolled in, the mounting pressure in her core dissipated.

Her eyes shot open.

It wasn't fear that made her lurch upward to a sitting position. Sarah'd had weeks to process the looming end of days. She chucked the vibrator on the floor where it rattled around like a defunct toy, and her cheeks flushed—not with terror but with rage.

Just one more orgasm ruined by the ineptitude, the arrogance, the *audacity* of men.

One more in a long line of disappointments.

Outside, tires squealed. That bitch, Wendy–the neighbor who complained to the HOA about her driveway pavers, Sarah just knew it had been her––shrieked and ran past the bedroom window. Footsteps pounded up the path to the front door. A key scraped against the knob. *Todd. Goddammit, Todd.*

Sarah took a deep breath. Todd was to stay at the office. That was the plan. Jessica and Ashleigh (Sarah hated that spelling. *Hated* it. But Todd insisted) were to stay at school. There'd be no sense dying alone on the highway trying to get everyone home. Better to go on as normal until it wasn't. That's what they'd agreed on.

The front door creaked on its hinges.

"Honey?" Todd called from the foyer.

Sarah threw the blanket off her legs and managed to slide to the bathroom and lock herself in before Todd could make it down the hall. Faintly, she heard the vibrator still hopping around on the tile.

Buddap-buddap-bzz.

"Honey?"

Buddap-buddap-bzz.

Sarah pressed her back against the door, gathering her legs in a hug. Stubble pricked at the tender skin of her forearms.

"You in here?"

She'd considered shaving last night, but what was the point? To look sexy in her coffin? No, there'd be no coffin, no funeral. No one left to bury her.

Sarah had decided to die with hairy legs.

Buddap-buddap–

The vibrator clicked off. Sarah winced as she imagined it in Todd's meaty paws.

Beside her left eye, the knob jiggled.

"Don't come in," she said.

It jiggled harder. "Honey, what's going on? Are you alright?"

Sarah shifted, feeling the slickness between her thighs. She eyed the scissors on the bathroom counter.

"You okay? Let me in!"

Let me in. Let me in. How many times had Sarah heard that? Jessica or Ashleigh or both in chorus? How many times had she been asked, *You okay?* with a tone that said, *don't answer that.*

That bitch Wendy rounded the corner of her yard, a flash of red curls beyond the sheer curtain. She was still screaming, and the light that poured in from outside dimmed, choked by the roiling wave of dust they'd been warned was coming. Weeks of tweets and TikToks. Noise, noise, noise strangling her feeds.

"Sarah?"

Todd never used her name, not in years anyway. At some point she'd been reduced to a pet name in exclusivity, in perpetuity, a change she never agreed to, but let pass by, one of the million blinks that blended together into the long sleep that was her marriage.

"What are you doing here?" The words slipped out in place of what she'd intended, dripping with vitriol. On any other day she would've been milder, would've masked her displeasure. But not today. Not when she'd been so fucking *close*.

"I came home to…" The end of Todd's thought was replaced by an earnest thud against the door that made Sarah jump. She leapt to her feet, and wasn't sure what she was thinking when she grabbed the scissors and brandished them like a knife. Another thud knocked chips of paint from the door frame, and on the third, the hardware bent, the lock failed, and Todd came tumbling in, huffing.

Even with her back pressed to the window, Sarah knew the dust cloud had thickened from the darkness around her. Still, flecks of eggshell white speckled on Todd's alcohol-swollen cheeks, glittering in the remaining daylight. The whites of his eyes looked all the more jaundiced by comparison, and the sallow yellow bulbs widened when he noticed the weapon in Sarah's hand.

"What the fuck are you—"

"What are *you* doing?" Sarah's eyes darted to the scissors and back. Her hand was not shaking. It was perfectly still. "What are you doing *here*?"

"I came home to–"

"To what?!" Sarah was screaming now, but not the high pitched yelp she'd heard from Wendy, hers was a low, throaty sound.

"To catch you flicking your bean, I suppose." Todd barked a thoughtless laugh.

A beat passed. A moment in time measured by the shrinking pitch of Wendy's cries.

Sarah didn't know what she was thinking when she plunged the scissors into Todd's chest. They stayed right where she put them, those two shiny handles suspended in the air. The dark stain started small, then spread out, painting Todd's baby-blue polo in a midnight winter color palette. Near-black indigo at the center bled into mulberry. Would she call it mulberry? Maybe the shade was more like wine. They watched it bloom together, and the irony didn't escape Sarah that this might be the first thing they'd done as a couple since–

"What the fuck, Sarah?" Todd dropped to his knees, then let out a yowl. Old football injury, Sarah remembered. His knees were never good, and from the clapping sound they made against the faux marble tile...

"Was it too much to ask?" Sarah walked a semi circle around her sputtering husband. "To get a few goddamn hours of peace and quiet at the end of the fucking world?"

Todd's mouth opened. His tongue moved and his lips formed shapes. But no sound escaped, like an infant imitating mama.

From the doorway, Sarah spotted the vibrator: a teal stripe on the pilled, floral bedspread. "I think I want a divorce," she said without looking at him.

Todd sucked in a gurgling breath. "Crazy bitch." His too-thick hands floundered around the scissors in his chest, fingers dancing over the handles, like he thought it might be a good idea to remove them, then thought better of it, cycling over and over on repeat. Delicate flicks of his fingertips over the shiny steel, nearly a strumming motion, and Sarah had the strange thought that if Todd had been so tender with her in the bedroom, she might not have had to wait until he left to *take a quick piss* to finish herself off.

Sarah crossed the room, clutching the teal, body-safe silicone in her palm. It was heavy. When she first got it, Todd had joked she needed a license to operate that kind of heavy machinery. Sarah hadn't laughed.

When she turned back, Todd struggled to his feet. Bracing himself on the doorframe, he held himself erect. "So this is how you want it to end?" he asked, the wine-colored stain now stretching its tendrils, engulfing a good three quarters of the polo.

Sarah couldn't help but think of how many bottles of peroxide it would take to remove a stain like that. Three, at least. Her nails dug into the satiny finish of the toy. "No," she said.

Todd gestured weakly at his injury. "What do you *want*?"

"I wanted it to end in quiet."

Todd shook his head with an incredulous curl of his mouth.

"I want–" she started, but stopped when she realized that was it.

I want.
I want.
I want.

He stepped toward her.

Sarah didn't remember deciding to swing the fist holding the vibrator, but she must've, because she heard that crack of body-safe silicone against flesh, then the smack of a meaty paw against faux marble tile. She saw a teal blur, then a sliver of white bone against pink and red sinew.

Sarah didn't count how many times she hit him.

Wendy had long stopped screaming, or perhaps she was screaming still, but in someone else's yard. Sarah's shoulder got tired, and when she looked up, there was no more light pushing through the sheer curtain; the dust cloud had brought an artificial night.

Sticky blood coated the vibrator's head, crowned by a film of gray particles that must have wriggled their way into the house through some imperceptible crack in a window. But she remembered from the packaging that it was water resistant. *Not waterproof, water resistant,* as she'd reminded herself so many times. Gingerly, she ran it beneath the faucet, digging her fingernails into the grooves until Todd's stain was thoroughly removed. Stepping over his body, she nestled herself back under the covers, her spot still warm.

Click.

More explosions were coming.

Buddap-buddap-bzz.

And Sarah let herself want.

You like that you dirty little...
You like that you dirty little...
You like that you dirty little...

A Curse in the Midnight Zone

From the glittering surface to the middle place where the sun still dapples her tawny flesh, my lover returns to me, voiceless, letting the midnight zone dim her features with an inky cast. She grasps the slime slicked stone to steady herself, ridiculous appendages flapping uselessly behind her.

"You're back." My tentacles loop and curl in the water, a shade darker than the absence of light. A gentle current lifts my hair, scarlet strands wrapping around my neck, tangling in the plunge between my breasts before drifting behind me.

Please, she mouths. Pathetic.

Still, I reach for her. Her cheek is leathery. Too much time up there.

Please.

Pruned fingertips trace the line of my chin, and I can't help that my eyes ease shut. For a moment, her touch is a salve, calming the acidic betrayal that ravages my insides. I enclose her in my many legs, feeling her shoulders drop, her muscles relax as I hold her. A flurry of tiny bubbles tickle my neck as she plants kisses there. I can almost forget that she left. Almost.

She reaches down, arms slipping easily past my satiny flesh, and removes her fabrics, strange things that hold water like a prison. I watch the current capture them, magenta blobs swept away with the tide.

Her legs part.

My cursed gift to her. The gift she begged for. The *curse* she begged for, spreading open now, pleading for something else, something familiar, another gift only I can give.

I weave my fingers into her golden hair. It gleams even here, where light itself is afraid to travel. My core tenses as her tongue flicks my earlobe.

One contraction of my limbs and we're propelled into my cave, the stone swallowing us just as her tight opening greedily swallows the tentacle I push inside.

Soundlessly, she gasps, drawing in water, drawing me deeper.

"Is this what you want?" I growl into her ear, positioning a sucker over her most sensitive place.

Nails drag across my back. Her grip tightens.

I grant her wish, thrusting inside her, the movements of her body and the lines of her face telling me exactly how to push her over the edge. This perversion of her form might be new–split legs in place of her slender tail–but our love is old, and I would know her desire if it came to me in the form of a crab, a ship, an anchor.

She reaches the peak of her pleasure with a shudder, collapsing against me; and I lay her down on the patch of kelp where I rest. Her chest rises and falls in time with the current, pulsing like the wisp of hair suspended in its pull. *I love you,* she mouths.

She's realized her mistake. Returned to me. What more can I ask?

I touch the place where her heart should be, breasts steadying as she calms. Pages appear, suspended in the water above. I catch a glimpse of where she signed her name, feel once more the way I broke that day before the contract tears, curls of paper caught in the water's pull swirling around us in a flurry. I imagine this must be what it's like on land, when they hold their–what did she call them? Parades? Confetti streaming from the sky when—

A shriek. Her nose screws up as the skin of her legs is torn and sloughed off by saltwater.

Her eyes go wide. With joy? Pain?

And her beauty is revealed, shimmering scales as golden as her hair seal the unnatural split, joining her limbs as her tail reforms. Her flat, useless teeth sharpen to points, better to tickle my neck, better to hunt with, better to—

"No." She grabs her throat as if she's surprised by the sound.

A shock of anguish snakes up my chest, but I push it down. "No?"

Her hands run frantically over her tail, as if to confirm it's not just an illusion. "What have you done?"

It's anger.

It's anger in her eyes.

"You—"

She returned to me. Realized her mistake—

"Change me back!"

I shrink into the corner, renewed agony as sharp as that first day when she came begging, reeking of shame. She cannot mean it. "I thought…" My voice catches. "Why did you come back?"

"I missed you." She barks a laugh, but there's no joy in it. "I didn't think you'd go back on your word."

"Me?" It's laced with more vitriol than I intend, but there's no stopping the flood of fury. "You debased yourself, bent into alien shapes to fit a world not meant for you, and I helped you do it! You—"

Broke my heart.

"I have a life there." With a flick of her tail she rises to her full height, crossing her arms over her chest. "It's not for you to judge."

I snicker. "As if *I* am the one consumed by judgment." My tentacles embrace my midsection. It's easier to jab at her, easier than feeling the bottomless emptiness.

"We had a deal." Her slim features give even this attempt at strength an air of vulnerability, and I can't help the urge to give her what she wants, no matter the cost to either of us, but the rules are clear.

"It's been rescinded." I flick away a curl of paper that's settled on my collarbone. A creeping dread chills me as I come to understand what this means, and the smugness falls away from her expression, as I expect she does too. "If you want to return, it will be at a higher price."

I close the space between us. If I could just make her understand, make her feel what I feel—

"Name it."

"It doesn't have to be like this." I reach for her arm but she withdraws. "We could be together, you and me. Who cares what anyone thinks?"

"I do." Her eyes pass over the stony walls. "This is not a life."

I dart through the water to capture her gaze. "It needn't be here! We could go anywhere, wherever you'd like!"

"And be gawked at?" She scoffs, shaking her head. "Change me back."

The taste of iron settles on my tongue, and I dislodge the fang embedded in my cheek. "Is it really so much better, up there?" I flail upward with such force, kelp rises from its spot before wafting back down. "You're a ghost of yourself, unable to talk and joke, unable to swim, your body mutated. Tell me you don't miss the sea."

Miss me.

She shoves me away, moving to the lips of the cave, where the faintest light can find her. "It's my choice."

My belly drops like a stone. She's heard every speech I can conjure, every assurance that her family might come around, in time. That the joy we'd find together would far outweigh the odd, skulking stare. "Coward." I say it low, but know she hears me.

"You should be ashamed." She sneers, pointed teeth visible between her curled lips.

"You're quite ashamed enough for the both of us." I puff my chest, spreading my tentacles as far as they'll reach. I'll not allow the small-minded to prevent my taking up space.

"It's not right," she says, voice cracking, "what we do." The words are not her own, borrowed from the mouths of neighbors, of family. "I only came because…" Her eyes trace the silty floor as if she might find the answer there. "Because I'm weak. But *he* loves me."

I sputter out a laugh. "He loves your silence."

"They accept me up there, as I was. I have a place."

"You had to carve yourself up to fit that place."

"You did the carving."

I rush to her side, turning her by the shoulders to face me. "You begged me."

Her inner lids flick closed. "And you obliged."

"Because I thought you would be happy." I coil my tentacles around her waist, hoping somehow the pressure might make her listen, make her hear me. "But you cannot be, because you came back. Were you happy? Tell me!"

"I'm better than this." She spits the words. "This *sin*."

"Fuck you."

I slump. Outcroppings in the rock scrape my back, but I don't care. For a moment, the only sound is the distant crunch of sand in the beaks of passing squid.

She clears her throat, fists balled at her sides. "Witch of the Water," her voice has taken on a formal tone, "I come requesting a bargain."

No. I'm drawn back to her despite myself, pulled by duty. I hover before her as if she's some passing merman wanting a sharper spear, some maid who dreams of ruling as queen, as if she's not the gravity around which my world spins. "Are you willing to pay the price?" I don't want to say it. I don't want to offer. But the rules are clear.

"I am."

At this, the contract appears, strobing bioluminescence from its pages.

"What is your wish?" Within my mind, I'm screaming, *Why isn't it me? Why am I not enough for you?*

"I wish to walk on land as people do." As she speaks, the words are etched, ink indigo and green like an oil slick.

"The price is high." The price is always high, just not usually for me. And though I wish with every barnacle crusted to the cave's wall that she would relent, refuse the bargain, she has watched me make countless deals, knows just what to say.

"I am willing to pay."

It occurs to me then, the final card I have to play. Perhaps it will convince her this is madness. Her shame cannot be so great that she would give up any possibility of—

"In light of the return of your previous gift, I have additional terms." The clause appears in ink with every word I speak. "Should you accept, you may never return to my lair, no matter the outcome of your little misadventure, no matter what this human man does or does not do to you. I may love you, but I am the Witch of the Water, and I am not to be trifled with."

My breath stills as she absorbs what I've said, this ultimatum. Too long she's flitted on the cusp of accepting what she is, what *we* are. Too many times she's shattered me to pieces, only to change her mind, then shatter me again. I'd bluff, if I could, but the clause is already written, ink the color of a bruise.

She remains silent, so I go on. "Should you agree, it will be the last word you speak, for your voice is mine to keep. In exchange, I will split your tail once more, give you legs to walk on. But understand that by baiting me, by using me to fulfill your true desire, then rebuffing me…"

Her eyelids tremble, a sure sign she's felt a rush of emotion, but restrains its expression. A flash of hope grants me strength to continue.

"If you're determined to spend your days with that man, though you do not love him, though I offer my love freely and know you freely love me in return, if you insist on walking a world not meant for you, when we could share one here, when I would gift you anything, pay for it with chunks of my body; if none of that might convince you, to let us love one another… Well, you'll rend my heart to pieces, and I will require yours as a replacement."

My lover fingers the water in front of her, stirring a cloud of plankton. "Take it," she says, in a childlike whisper. "It is already yours." She does not meet my eyes.

My tentacles go stiff. My spine turns to jelly as she reaches for the contract and signs, letters too big and beautiful for their meaning.

"Very well." My hand closes easily around her throat. Her scream dies as I rip the cords from her neck, bits of flesh muck up the surrounding water, illuminated by a faint green glow closing the hole in her flesh. One by one, I feed the tubes of cartilage into my gullet, crunching down the tough cords until they crack and give way between my teeth. She looks on with horror, thinly veiled by a determined frown. Frantically, she points at her chest, mouthing, *Take it! Take it, you witch!*

The strike shatters her ribcage. My fist grows warm as it plunges into her, shards of bone digging into my hand as I grasp the pumping organ. So deeply I have coveted it, this slimy, thumping thing. I let my fingers play between the ventricles, and my lover tosses her head back, once again mute, unable to articulate her pain. I rip. The organ comes out clean, water around us opaque with pieces of her, green light glowing brighter as it mends her chest.

Thump.

Her heart pumps within the safety of my hands.

Thump.

Her glorious tail tears at the center, scales falling into the water, swept away by the current like a thousand flashing minnows.

Thump.

I draw the organ to my own chest.

Silt flies up from the bottom as she kicks, grasps water with naked fingers, no webbing at all.

Thump.

She moves slowly toward the surface, and I bring her heart to my face.

Thump.

The beat massages my temple.

Thump.

She abandons the midnight zone, light dappling her tawny flesh.

Thump.

My lover joins with the glittering surface, and I press her heart to my eyes, to my lips, to my nose.

Thump.

I let it block out everything else, retreating to my lair.

Thump.

I bang hard on the stone walls, clutching the beating organ to my chest as the rocks fall in, sealing the entrance.

Thump.

Utter blackness.

Thump.

Emptiness.

Thump.

Quiet.

Backseat Driver

Published by *Shortwave Magazine*, October '22

A bleeding sun rears its angry head over the hills surrounding your childhood holler. You smudge a bit of dirt into your hairline and hurl your suitcase into the open trunk of your mother's silver van, Mark glaring at you between the headrests.

"Thought you were riding with Sadie."

"Yeah well," you scoff for good measure, "she bailed." The words are cold. Emotionless. You've rehearsed them a hundred times.

Your brother rights himself in the canvas seat. "Good for her."

He says it loud enough for you to hear, but you're too old to take the bait. No sense getting into it with Mark before the key's turned in the ignition. You're not kids anymore.

"Where are they?"

Mark clicks on his Kindle. "Just grabbing the last few bags. Eager for some carpool karaoke or what?"

You slide into the backseat, already feeling motion sickness creep in like cold breath on the back of your neck. *Never take the chick's car*, you remind yourself. *Never again.*

Susan and Roger Gladwell–dear old Mom and Dad– emerge from your colonial childhood home, weighed down by bulging luggage, their steps made more tedious by smacking flip flops.

"Oh, honey, look!" your mother says, as if you can't hear her. "Jimmy decided to join us after all." You hear her grin, though the view is obscured by your old gym bag: reclaimed, overstuffed, and slung across her arms.

"It's James," you mutter.

The van bucks as your father tosses heavy bags into the back one by one.

"Watch it!" you say.

"Oh Roger, be more careful, Hun. Jimmy could have something breakable in there. You didn't pack anything fragile, did you, sweetie?"

Your eyes roll. You picture *Acqua di Gio* saturating your already stained clothes as it spills from a shattered bottle. "I'm thirty, Mom. Of course I packed–" Your mother's rustling makes you turn. She's clearing a path to your bag. "Just leave it."

She reaches for the zipper. "I'll just do a quick check and then–"

"Leave it, I said."

Your mother takes one of her big breaths in, and slams the trunk shut. Your father can barely fit in the driver's seat with his giant map in both hands. *Typical*, you think.

"Dad, there's no need for that. GPS comes standard these days."

Susan perks up her curls with a few bats of her palms. "Oh sweetie, you know your father."

You picture back roads with bumps and potholes, U-turns, and winding mountain roads. There's a roiling in your stomach. "I got it," you say.

Leaning over the center console, you mash a few buttons on the touchscreen. Despite preferring the old-fashioned way, your dad offers up the address, and within seconds the screen reads, *Calculating Route*.

"Well, that's what I was doing!" Roger jokes.

Susan gives a perfunctory chuckle.

"Just trust me, Dad."

Tennessee summer battles the blowing AC for dominance as quiet moments tick by.

"Should be any second," you say.

The little red wheel spins round and round on the screen, and the message changes. *System Update.*

"Can I put on the radio while we–" Susan starts.

"Just a minute." The last thing you need is her interrupting the reboot. "We could sit here an hour and we'd waste less time than we would following that map. What's it from, the 90s? Do they even sell those anymore?"

"Well of course they do–"

A crisp voice with a slight Alabama drawl interrupts your mom and punches you in the gut. *"Welcome to voice command navigation."*

I am joining you on this trip, one way or another.

"Damn, that sounds familiar," Mark says, looking up from his Kindle.

No, no, you insist to yourself. "It's just a preset. I'm sure there's lots of voices you can choose from." You reach for the screen, but your dad waves you back to your seat.

"Let's just get on the road," he says. He might be right. The further you get from here, the better.

Susan buckles her seatbelt. "So glad you decided to join us after all, Jimmy."

"Didn't have much of a choice." Mark is wearing that sly smile that makes you want to squeeze his throat. "His girl dumped him."

"She didn't–"

"I'm so sorry to hear that." Your mother flashes a sympathetic smile via the rearview mirror as the van pulls out of the long drive. Let her believe what she wants. It's no use getting into who dumped who.

"Left turn on Maple Leaf St. 200 feet ahead."

"Well, I knew that," your dad says.

"It's like I always say," your mother continues, "What's meant to be, will be!"

"Right." You gaze out the window, knowing you'll be fine once you get on the highway and leave all these back roads behind.

"Stay on the current road for two miles."

"I swear, that voice is so familiar." Mark looks to the van's upholstered ceiling as if he might find the answer there. Your abs clench. You hope he doesn't.

Susan busies herself surfing radio stations until she finds 109.6: Best of the Oldies. At the next rest stop, you'll get your headphones from your bag. You should've thought of that before you got going. Now it's going to be soft rock for the next hour.

"This is so wonderful," Susan says, watching pine trees whip by the window. "Must be twenty years since we've been on a family trip. She grins wide enough for you to see her sparkling metal fillings from the backseat. Then she catches herself. "So sorry to hear about Sadie though. She sounded like a lovely girl. I'm sure it's for the best." She smoothes her floral blouse.

"Her loss," you say.

"I'm sorry, I didn't understand that."

Susan's hand hovers over the navigation screen, where once again a red circle spins.

"Left turn ahead."

Your father yanks the steering wheel, barely catching the turn in time. "You'd think it'd give us a little more heads-up than that!"

"Just keep an eye on the screen." You remember that two-hour trip to Dollywood that ended up taking four. And your mother wonders why it's been twenty years since you agreed to a road trip.

Mark tucks his Kindle beneath your mom's seat and starts flipping through his phone. You rest your head against the window. It's chilled from the blowing AC, and the cold burrows into your temple like a termite, like a maggot laying eggs, stabilizing the rising motion sickness. You close your eyes, thinking you might be able to nap, sleep away the twistiest part of the trip and wake once you're on the highway.

"It is her!" Mark's eyes gape with petty delight. He yanks his headphones off and thrusts the phone to where your mother can see. "Check this out." With a tap, Sadie's voice fills the car.

Your entrails do a polka inside you, and you'd shit yourself if not for the firm clench you've got on your ass. Sadie's rose-gold hair whips back and forth as she dances on the recording, her voice emanating from the tiny speaker.

"Don't be a creep, Mark!" You lunge for him, but your seatbelt's safety lock keeps your hand inches from the phone.

"Does Sadie do voice acting or something? You gotta admit, Mom. Same voice, isn't it?"

Your mother's eyes narrow as she listens, but you do your best to drown out the recording. "Don't be a jackass. Doesn't even sound like her," you say.

"What?" Mark rapid-fire presses the volume button and starts the Tik-Tok again.

Sadie calls out from the phone, "*Top ten reasons–*"

"Dude, stop!" You lunge again, this time dislodging the phone from his hand. Mark erupts into raucous laughter, just like he did when you were kids.

"Wait for it, wait for it. There's a turn coming up!"

"*In eight-hundred feet, turn right onto 1-86 North.*"

"That's her, bro!"

"Boys, boys." Your mother waves you into silence. "Let's all just relax now. How about a game?"

You draw your arms tight across your chest. Mark retrieves his phone, confident he's rattled you, and resumes his scrolling. Roger eases the minivan onto the highway.

Should be a straightaway for at least fifty miles. You settle, knowing your brother might be a jackass, but at least you avoided puking out the window and soiling your last clean pair of pants.

"In one mile, take the exit onto Marrowbone Dr."

"What?" Your father bats at the navigation screen with no effect. "That can't be right."

"Hazard ahead. You are on the fastest route."

"I don't think that's right." His bushy brows furrow, shot through with gray.

"It's right."

Roger's fingers tighten around the wheel. He whispers, "Did it just answer me?"

"It's voice activated, dad." Mark smirks.

"Hmm." Your father eyes the screen with suspicion.

"What a wonder of a thing," your mother says.

The turn signal clicks, and Roger merges into the right lane to take the exit.

"Take the exit," the GPS croons.

Mark is right. It does sound like Sadie.

Sounds just like me.

Though it's only a few miles from home, Marrowbone isn't an area you frequent. Never was. But lately it's been pulling you in, hasn't it? Its dense woods like strong, grasping fingers. The roadside sign tells you there's only one gas station, 1.5 miles to the right.

"Turn left onto Marrowbone Dr."

Your father abides.

Apart from the highway tearing it in half, you're surrounded by forest on all sides. Pines and evergreens tower around you. Old trees. Trees that were here before you. Will remain after you.

"Stay on the current road."

Between the branches, you spot the odd house. Tucked behind heavy iron gates, rusted and chained, they sport sagging roofs, chipped paint, cars on concrete blocks in the yard. A burly black dog snaps at a chainlink fence, foam dripping from its snarling maw.

"You are on the fastest route."

"Didn't the Jepsens move to Marrowbone a ways back?" your mother asks.

Your father nods, both hands still wrapped around the wheel.

"This must lead back to the highway," your mother says. She pats your father's thigh. He mutters agreement.

A red building ahead catches your eye. *Shorty's Tavern.* Nausea, or is it fear, rears up like a cornered stag.

"I think we should turn back," you say, hand to your lips.

"You are on the fastest route," the GPS responds.

"You heard the lady," Roger says, pleased with his joke.

Saliva pours into your mouth. "No, really," you eke out. "Let's get back to the highway. I think I'm gonna be sick." Perspiration beads on your forehead, but it's not the sickness screaming at you to turn back the way you came.

"GPS said there was an accident or something. I'm sure if we just keep going, we'll loop right–"

"In 500 feet, turn right onto 7th Place."

"See?" Your mother's tone is light. Always light. "It's bringing us right back now."

Gravel crunches beneath the tires as your father turns onto 7th.

"The highway is the other direction," you say, sweat seeping into the fabric of your collar.

"The road must curve, sweetie. Just relax. Look out the window."

Your mother rifles through her purse in search of a peppermint, just like she has since you were a child. Though it won't ease your sickness. Not this time.

You pass that powder blue mailbox on the left. It's the same one. Yes.

"Pull over."

Roger guides the van onto the slim shoulder, and hot Tennessee air pushes against you as you throw open the heavy door. You retch, stumbling toward the back of the van. Last thing you need is Mark mocking you. Hands on your knees, you pull a slow breath through your nose. You clench your stomach. *Either puke, or let's get the fuck out of here,* you think.

Nothing comes. You wipe your face, and from inside the vehicle you hear my voice.

"150 feet northwest, and you will arrive at your destination."

Bile singes your throat as the voice comes out in staccato bursts. Should've stopped to have breakfast. We could've had a nice, leisurely breakfast, but instead…

"150 feet northwest, and arrive at your destination," I say again.

When you return to the van, Susan and Roger are already deep in discussion about glitches and faulty programming. Mark is handing your father his map.

"150 feet northwest, and you arrive at your destination," I insist.

"Turn the damn thing off," you croak.

Your mother pokes at the screen, but I won't be silenced.

"150 feet northwest, between the boulder and the hemlock. Just beneath a spider's web. You will arrive at your destination."

"Fuckin' weird," Mark says, staring at the screen. The digital map shows nothing but white dappled with green for trees.

"Proceed on foot. Estimated time of arrival, 6:53am."

"We should check it out." He's popped open his door before you can say a word.

"Mark Aaron, have you lost your mind?" your mother says, fiddling with her seatbelt.

"Come on, Mom! You wanted family fun. It's like one of your mystery shows. What is it? Poirot? Where's your sense of adventure?"

"Shut the fuck up, Mark. I feel like shit. We're not about to prancing through the woods because of some technical glitch."

"Boys!" Your mother unbuckles her seatbelt. "You know what? I would like to go."

Your father kills the engine and sighs.

"We need some family bonding. That much is *very* clear. And Jimmy?" She stares daggers into you. "You look like hot hell anyhow. Some fresh air and firm ground would do you good."

Your tongue searches for the right argument, but all it finds is a fungus gnat. You spit but it clings to your lip until you wipe it away.

"We'll all get some fresh air, solve a little mystery." Her brow dances up and down at your father who has joined her beside the culvert. "Have some family time. The whole point of this trip anyway."

"Excellent." Mark is beaming. "So, what'd she say?"

"150 feet northwest, between the boulder and the hemlock. Just beneath a spider's web. You will arrive at your destination."

Roger startles and stares back into the van. "Damn thing's off." His head shakes in confusion.

"Probably has a battery backup," Mark says. "Let's go! You heard the lady."

Can't be, you think. All trees look the same. And you were one town over. Weren't you?

"Proceed to your destination. You are on the fastest route."

Mark jogs toward his best guess at northwest, and your mother summarizes the latest episode of Poirot as she struggles to keep up in her flip flops. Your father lingers behind them, just a few steps ahead of you. His eyes hesitate over a spot on your neck. You reach up out of instinct, feel the deep scratch still bruising around the edges.

"Come on, slowpokes!" she calls. She's really getting into the spirit of it, solving a real life mystery. The mystery of what happened to Sadie Grover.

To me.

Minutes pass. The trail thins, gnarled boughs reaching for you with sappy appendages. Clustered leaves knit closer together, choking the light as it tries to force its way through the tree cover. Daylight strangled. A branch clips your shoulder. Dull pain radiates from the fresh, hidden bruise.

"Alright, nothing here," you proclaim. "Let's turn back."

But you're too late.

"What's this?" Your mother has already spotted it.

Just ahead, a pile of freshly turned soil, an aberration against the carpet of pine needles.

You should've thought of that, really.

"Let's go!" It's a demand this time, one that makes your father turn on his heel.

"Don't speak to your mother that way, Jimmy."

"It's James. It's James, goddammit!"

Susan's eyes seek answers in the powdery dirt, the same dirt embedded in your fingernails. Roger's steely blue eyes silence you, but Mark crouches beside the mound.

"Oh shit." He clasps his palm over his nose. You think about running, but the keys are clipped to your father's belt loop. Where would you go? "I think it's a…"

Your mother does the Sign of the Cross, and your father is quick to wrap an arm around her and turn her from the morbid sight.

You hesitate.

You're not ready to see me again.

"You have arrived at your destination." My voice booms from the trees, from the hidden corners of your mind, from within my shallow grave.

Mark clears the thin layer of soil from my face. My eyes are wide like you left them, dirt caked to blood-red sclera. "Jesus Christ." He has no clever quips now. It's Mark's turn to retch. His vomit joins with my bodily fluids, seeping deep into the earth. It's a mess down there: piss and shit and a masticated Wendy's breakfast sandwich. More food for the maggots already sniffing at my corpse.

Your pulse races, vision blurs.

"It's fucking Sadie." Mark's hoarse voice tells your parents what you already know.

Scratches burn fresh beneath your shirt. Blisters bubble on your soft palms. You're not used to digging, or any manual labor for that matter.

"Jimmy…" Your father's voice trails off. He would've been disappointed in you. In how winded you became, bursting every capillary in my eyeballs. Never kept up with that fitness routine he worked out for you in high school. But then, you've disappointed him in a lot of ways. This? Only the latest.

A smattering of flying insects hovers around my partially exposed form. They came to do the cleanup job you neglected. How does it feel? Less work ethic than a dung beetle. Our last argument returns to you in flashes. Squabbles with Mark pale in comparison. All that rage you hid from him, saved up for me. Unleashed on my swelling body in curses, taunts, and blows. You swore you never wanted to see me again. But now that you're here, you can't help but take those few steps forward.

I wear your handprints like a necklace. Jewelry of the dead.

It's a pleasure to meet your folks. Shame I look such a mess, but you can't blame me for that. That was all your doing.

Is it only you who hears me? Am I some strange nightmare from which you'll wake, sweaty?

Oh, but you are sweaty.

My scent reaches your nostrils, spoilt meat with a hint of almond. It draws you closer. You fixate. You scarcely hear your mother call 911.

Mark weeps for me. Tears that should've come from you.

Do you want to tell them? Or should I?

The secret between us rots in my belly, just where you left us.

Roger grabs the phone. "Yes, right away," he tells the operator. "Marrowbone." My words spring from his healthy throat. Your lips trace them in time.

"150 feet northwest, between the boulder and the hemlock. Just beneath a spider's web. You will arrive at your destination."

Write My Eulogy On The Gloryhole Bathroom Stall

Published by Dragon's Roost Press in *The Pleasure in Pain*, April 2024

I met god in the men's room at the corner of 4th and Broadway. I don't make a habit of using the men's room, but rain was coming in sideways, landing like bee stings onto my ear and neck. Did a quick one-two look. Didn't see the ladies'. So, I ducked inside, just wanted a respite long enough to phone a rideshare.

My first fear—that I'd find a line of dudes, dicks out, piss streaming—was unfounded. The bathroom sat empty. Empty except for the smell. I slapped my palm to my face but couldn't cover it, urea and shit and stagnant water so thick it turned the air viscous. I whipped out my phone, determined to grab a car and get the fuck out of there, but I moved too quick and dropped it. Of course I dropped it. And it went careening across the yellow tile, little one inch squares framed by more filth than grout. It slid into the corner stall, and I wiggled my fingers as I caught up to it, as if I might get ahead of the germs I was about to touch, shake 'em off before they clung to me.

The fluorescent bulb overhead flickered: one, two, three. It was eerie, in that horror-movie-gearing-up-to-the-killing-scene sort of way. But I wrote the goosebumps off to the lasting chill of freezing rain, averted my eyes from the abomination in the toilet, and leaned into that too cramped corner where my phone glowed.

Face turned away from the thing responsible for one third of the smell, I was eye to eye with the wall, and looking back, it must've been god that dropped the deuce in there, turned my chin toward the graffitied wall; because if not for that, I wouldn't have found it.

A hole.

It was about the size of a fist, and deep as anything from what I could tell. Inside was that black-black, that absence of light black, where you can't tell how far it goes. Could've been Mariana's fucking trench in there. I don't know what it was, a calling maybe, but something made me reach. While my left hand secured my phone in my jeans pocket, my right slipped into the hole, careful not to touch the sides. I felt for the stud, the insulation, something, but I was halfway to my elbow and when a pinch made me yank it back. A bug, a spider, a snake, maybe? Three red divots in my knuckles and a pulsing feeling. I knew I'd been bit, and I would've gotten the hell out of there, I would've, if not for what followed.

What began as a pinch rolled to my elbow then armpit. It wrapped around my neck and spread through my core. I didn't realize I'd landed on my ass until my hands jumped to brace me from sprawling; but even as I felt mystery grime flake beneath my fingernails, I didn't care.

To call it a *high* would be to trivialize it.

There are seven wonders of the world, people say, and I became the eighth. For the first time, the creator of the universe looked right at me, looked right at me *approvingly*. The rain outside became the constant heartbeat of the world, the fear of germs faded with the recognition that no lifeform was truly apart from myself.

Time slipped; the separation between the atoms of my flesh and air around me dissipated. My body and spirit swelled with peace and warmth, enveloping and smothering every painful thing. It was a state of being so close to how I'd heard religious folk imagine heaven, and yet so much more and outside of understanding that again the descriptor falls short. And I sat alone beside the gloryhole bathroom stall, alone with god, and it was certainly good.

***

My phone was dead and the rain had stopped when reality returned. If anyone came in, I didn't notice. Meeting god must've stretched me somewhere inside, because while I didn't have the dull ache in my head of a hangover, I had the prickling anxiety of a new space opened up beneath my rib cage, and a vacancy there that itched deeper than skin and nerve.

I didn't catch a ride share. I walked home.

Night air was cool and crisp. The storm had dumped all the humidity from the air into the streets. My breaths were easy but shallow. Each step drew me further from 4th and Broadway. I stopped several times. Considered going back. But I figured Alyssa would be worried, a notion confirmed when I slipped through our apartment door to find her pacing and frantic.

"Where the *fuck* have you been? I've been calling."

I held up my phone screen, rapid pressing the buttons to no effect.

"Shit, I was worried."

"Sorry, I—"

"What happened to your hand?"

I glanced down to find the bite marks had turned from red pricks to angry, purple vines clutched around my palm. "Bug bite, or something. I think." My voice sounded distant, even to me, and Alyssa pressed.

I tried to explain what had happened.

"You must've gotten stuck by a needle. Lucky as shit you didn't overdose. Actually, Sam, we should get you checked out, just in case." She moved to where her coat hung on the wall.

"No, no." I dropped my purse on the counter. "I'm fine, just need some sleep."

She only argued for five minutes more before surrendering to the bathroom to brush her teeth. I rehearsed lines over and over in my head, but couldn't come up with a way to get her to go back with me, not tonight. The empty space beneath my ribs hummed as I settled into bed. I had to go back. To be with god. To feel unburdened and wholly seen. But I told myself it could wait until tomorrow, when Alyssa was rested and her curiosity might get the best of her.

Uneasily, we slept.

***

In the men's room at 4th and Broadway, Alyssa clutched her hand over her nose, just like I had.

"Christ, Sam."

"Just look."

I tugged her by her shirt sleeve, candy pink against the jittery fluorescent glow of dying bulbs and grime-yellow tile. She squinted to read the graffiti surrounding the hole.

"*Margret Ashbury is a whore. Dylan: Fridays 6-7pm, suck & fuck.* Very nice, Sam."

A flash of impatience made me bite back a retort, but my eye caught the words scribbled in red sharpie beneath the gloryhole. *The devil made me cum.*

"I see it, okay? Your hand looks… we need to get you to a doctor. What if a black widow was hiding in there? You could have sepsis or something."

"Please, just try it. I can't explain it, I've already tried. There's no way you can understand unless you——"

"Hep C. HIV. Sam, no fucking chance I'm putting my hand in there. I humored you, alright? I came, I smelled, I saw it. Let's fucking go."

The vacant space inside my ribs seemed to expand like heated air, a void that screamed without sound. I wanted to reach behind the wall, to grasp for more, but I let Alyssa walk me out, I even agreed to lunch and pretended to listen when she brought up that coworker who steals snacks from the communal fridge again. Better if she didn't realize, I figured. Would make it easier to sneak back.

The thirty-five minute lunch seemed to stretch on, an infinite purgatory of watching my lover butter bread, draw soup to her lips spoonful by too-small spoonful, sip sprite, ice cubes clinking against her teeth.

"I'm not hungry, really," I told Alyssa, I told the waitress.

I offered my card before the waitress brought the bill, and as I signed the check, the lie came out like a song. "Totally forgot, promised I head into work for a few."

Suspicion crinkled her freckled nose. "Thought you were off today."

"I am." I got up. "New hire, helping to get him oriented. Rob, lives with his mom type, not gonna last."

Alyssa shrugged and her expression relaxed. I leaned across the table for a parting kiss, half wondering how I conjured Rob so quickly, half walking the route back to 4th and Broadway in my mind.

The walk was an impatient blur. When my fingers met the metal door handle, the aching void in my sternum nearly ripped my breastbone in half. I rolled my sleeve to the elbow, cherishing the moments just before my fist disappeared into the dark. Seconds ticked by like sludge as I waited, eager for the little prick and the ecstasy that followed.

Then, the slice that made me cry out. I yanked my arm back out of instinct, but bliss gobbled me up before I had time to observe the injury. And it didn't matter anymore. I floated. Everything was fine. God spoke.

Does it hurt? He asked. *You're doing so well. Does it hurt?*

"Yes," I mumbled.

A slump brought me flat down, my sandal sliding off my foot.

I want more, god said.

"Of me?" The words rolled over my lolling tongue.

Give me more of you.

I dragged myself across the tile, inch by impossible inch, eyes rolling and vision blurred. My head grew too heavy, flopped to one side. I tossed a crooked arm toward the hole, and almost thought I saw empty space where the tip of my pinky usually was.

I probably saw it.

But it didn't matter.

My aim floundered, hand missing the hole entirely, but my elbow managed to make it into the black, and no sooner had I offered it did god accept it, hot agony racing up my nerves, fingertip to armpit.

The most delicious emptiness chased all thoughts and pain away. Only a throbbing remained. It traveled through my blood. It gathered in my center. It congealed between my thighs. God wanted me, intimately, vulnerably. And I wanted to offer myself. In the flickering fluorescent light, I removed my top, let it fall, and when the hem dipped into the toilet, my fingers raced to my pussy instead of to save it. I pressed my left breast against the hole, working myself into a frenzy. I thought of god's teeth. I thought of razored bicuspids, sharpened as only a deity's might be, piercing my areola, shredding the membranes beneath.

I moaned.

The slickness of my pussy lips let my hand slip inside, slowed only by the constraints of my jeans.

"Come on," I said, breathy, impatient, arching my back to press my breast further into the hole. The pressure built with the anticipation, wetness bleeding through my jeans as I kept the rhythm, anxiously awaiting the slice.

Is this a gift?

"Yes," came out like a plea.

I'd already started coming when god freed my nipple from the bounds of my flesh.

There was everything, then: The stinging, the shuddering climax, the gentle oblivion.

I collapsed onto the tile. Life-warmth poured down my stomach, my jeans were stained burgundy, and I checked my hand to find my little finger missing and gore flowing from elbow to wrist.

But it didn't matter.

I took a deep breath.

I laid flat.

I studied the water stains on the ceiling.

I let my fingers trace the graffiti.

I hooked my nail into a hardened piece of gum affixed to the toilet paper dispenser.

"Can I stay like this forever?" My voice sounded dreamy, and god didn't answer. I let myself be held by something which had called to me. Maybe all my life it had called to me. And I knew that nothing had ever felt right until this. I didn't go back to Alyssa's.

***

My remaining days were hazy. Alyssa kept calling, my parents kept calling, my boss kept calling. There was knocking sometimes, and I got good at being quiet. Very quiet, until it stopped.

Alyssa texted. She said lots of things. Things about losing. Losing her. She named a lot of other things, which didn't matter.

Then nobody was calling. And that was good.

The first time god fucked me, he wasn't gentle. It wasn't a romance in any way I'd seen or experienced, but the seduction burned hot and fast and desperate. I'd pulled my jeans and panties down, and pressed my pussy right up against the hole like a dog. I wanted to feel god's tongue. I wanted it to plunge inside me, to rip out my cervix with its barbed tip, to gush come and blood until the writing on the bathroom stall was washed away with my liquid, depraved pleasure.

God took my other nipple, my left thumb, my right hand to the wrist.

God had a fat cock and a warm pussy.

I fucked and I got fucked, I gave and I got and I gave pieces away. The pain was gone, even as the blood soaked through my tattered clothing, dried and crusted and flaked off every part of me. Even as I came so hard I pissed myself. Even when hunger had me so weak I passed out, it didn't matter. God was all I needed, god's gifts were abundant and if there was still a world outside that heavy metal door, it didn't need me anymore. And I didn't need it. I'd given Alyssa a chance. I'd tried to show her. Yes, it wasn't my fault she couldn't see. And now she'd never know. She'd never know *him*. She'd never know the fullness of being empty.

Fuck Alyssa.

I squatted in front of god's hole and gave him my ass.

I knew the freedom of giving myself selflessly, of receiving gratefully, of lightening as I was unburdened of my intestines. They made the sound of slop as they went coiling onto the yellow tile. God slurped them up like spaghetti. One long pull and they raced into the gloryhole like a speedy toy train, leaving a slick trail behind like smudged tracks. I'd never been so savored, my body like a sweet wine, ripe for consumption.

I dipped my fingers in dark liquid. On the bathroom door I scribbled, *Resplendent suffering*.

We had braided, god and pain and the cosmos and completion and never-having-been and my throbbing clitoris. And my flesh could not be parsed from the most intimate particles of the universe. No separation stood between me and the oldest suffering and the first pleasure. God fucked me into nothingness. I consumed carnality in its purest form as god drew my head to the glory hole and beyond it, took me into her pussy as his cock penetrated my throat. Clenching and thrusting and a kind, contented knowing.

God came.

And I blinked from being. A snap in which I relived my many years of existence and my very few days of living. I came to this one reflection:

If I'd have known that first rainy day what I know now. If I'd realized what would happen, how Alyssa would spend her birthday crying, how dad would never again hear a phone ring without a stitch of anxiety, that my body would rot on the yellow tiled floor for six days before anyone found me, that the insects would've chewed through my sclera, that shit leaked from my gaping anus at the end, and the mortician felt embarrassed for me and had to tell his wife about it just to throw off some of the shame, my shame. If I'd have known on that first rainy day, I would've shoved my hand into that hole even faster. I would've never taken it out.

Part II:

The Many Lives of Becca and Gem

Part II

The Many Lives of Becca and Gem

Mulberry Silk

Published by Nosetouch Press in *Fiends in the Furrows III*, August 2023

Becca curls her arm around our Intern, a waste of her delighted smiles and flashing eyes. He is one who comes to visit. We are those who came to stay. She knows he will be Indigo, as do I. Yet I watch her chatter from behind my steaming vat with palms stained plum. The wooden oar splinters as I stir, as I waft vapors into my own face. Dye so thick it invites a person to find its bottom.

"Don't overdo it," Oliver says. He stirs vermillion beside me.

Our Intern points and gawks. Stares at our towering looms like a fascinated bird. Sparrows blush with embarrassment from their high perches in the trees. Becca giggles, though I'm too far away to hear.

I followed her to The Collective. Eighteen miles off the exit, ten down a dirt road. Past the gorge and into the woods. An orange cottage with white trim on the left, the one with daisies in the rock garden. That's where we live now. Our first day I'd pressed my palm against our new home, been surprised by the chill of waved metal. Shipping containers. We live in a village of shipping containers, converted and stylized, not one the same as another. There's purple with teal trim, charcoal with red, one modern, one craftsman, one painted like wood. On a haphazard gravel street that twists and juts off to each property, for walking only. No cars allowed. *Exhaust ruins the dye,* The Widow had said. Not said, but wrote in a letter.

I slide my oar from the vat, scrape it on the side to spill as little plum as possible. I rest it against the vat and push the tin lid on top. Becca weaves her delicate fingers through the overhead loom. The Intern puffs his chest, leans into her while he talks. She is not thinking of me.

"Have you met her?" the Intern asks. He is a city person through and through, from his slicked hair down to his shiny leather shoes.

Becca rolls blonde hair between her fingers. "Not yet." She bats her lashes.

The Intern huffs. I hate him. "Do you think I might ... she's a legend in the fashion world."

"You won't." I'm upon them now, fixing my sour gaze on Becca, who straightens and glares back at me.

"You don't know that," she says.

I must stand between them. "How would you like to help prepare the leaves?"

The Intern's eyes grow wide. He's hungry. Desperate, bobbling his head in agreement.

Judy and Raul carry deep baskets overflowing with cuttings. Tina gathers mulberries in an aluminum box, the corners of her mouth stained plum like my hands. The leaves must be collected. Must be washed. The Widow has been clear. I show him how to pinch the stem, clip it clean between my nails, but he's clumsy. Yanks and tears. He does not belong here.

A few more days, I remind myself.

***

Two rubber bands wait for me on the wooden railing. I stretch the yellow one between my pointer finger and thumb. Dawn's light pushes its way through a blanket of fog that has settled around the lowermost branches of the Eastern Hemlocks. I spy Hendricks. He watches me with a crooked neck, his black feathers shining an oily blue. *Indigo*. Four peanuts wobble on the woodgrain.

"Good morning, Henricks."

He doesn't respond. Though we've struck this bargain—peanuts for rubber bands, or screws, or pieces of wire—he does not trust me. That is okay. He is a crow. I know this is his nature. It is not personal.

Becca didn't come home last night. I woke and I woke and I woke. 12 a.m. 2 a.m. 4. Her bedside cold. I imagine his grubby fingers pushing her golden hair behind her ear. His filthy claws pawing at her milky skin. This is her nature. But she is not a crow. It *is* personal.

Steam rises thick from the vats, blends with the falling fog. Oliver heats water in a kettle over a gas stove.

"Coffee?" he asks. He asks this every morning.

And every morning I say, "Yes."

It's instant. Quite terrible really. But I stir and I thank him. I've become accustomed to that. Stirring and lying.

"Have you seen Becca?"

He slurps, all ten fingers wrapped around the warm mug. "You two still fighting?"

I swallow the lump in my throat. "We're not fighting." Another lie. Becca is cross with me. She says it's because I cut my hair off. But I know the truth. It's because I love her too much.

"Well, better shake off all this weirdness soon. Only two more days. We need to bring our best selves." Oliver smooths his black hair over his ivory skin. Perfect for vermillion.

I nod.

One by one, naked, hanging bulbs illuminate the shipping container homes. The sun reaches further into the sky, burns up the fog. It's clear air all around us now. I can see high up into the thinning boughs. The owl nest is thicker than yesterday. Good on her. She works hard.

There's something wrong with Becca.

She wears a tunic dress, thin fabric over her hard nipples. It wafts around her, glad to be in her company. The Intern's hand is on the small of her back. I hate him. Goosebumps creep over my arms and thighs. Judy lays a wooden bowl in front of me. A fire ant snaps at my calf. Poison burns, but I'll live. It is good to hurt on the outside.

Mulberry leaves have ragged edges. They're shaped like palm-sized hearts. I chew and chew and chew, like a donkey gnawing cud. I feel the filmy green stain of chlorophyll on my teeth, viridian. That's not a color we're using this time. Indigo, vermillion, plum, burlywood, and mountbatten pink. I didn't know the last two. Had to sneak out in the middle of the night, dip white cotton into the vats to learn. My cheeks flushed with shame. If The Widow knew, she'd boot me out. Unacceptable not to know. Burlywood reminds me of khaki, a warm, sandy color. Mountbatten pink is more like purple, I'd say. But never out loud. Becca feeds The Intern who sneers while he chews. His sloshing saliva beats at my temples, a sharp pain worse than the fire ant bite. At the bottom of my bowl is a split leaf. This is her fault. A sign from the gods.

Two more days.

***

I wake sweating. I dreamt I caught Hendricks in a glue trap. His wings beat wild, and his eyes screamed, *Traitor!* I snapped his fragile neck. He finally spoke to me, and I popped his thin vertebrae in my twisting fist. Cold morning air chills my damp spine when I reach the porch. I run my hand along the bare wooden railing. No rubber bands. He knows. I whisper an apology. *I'm sorry, Hendricks. I didn't mean it.*

I must move on because today is the Ceremony. I wipe my tears on my forearm and join the coffee drinkers at the picnic tables. It hasn't rained in a week and the slits between my toes fill with grit, my sandals black with filth. Oliver can't stop smiling. I think his coffee might leak through his curled lips. His joy haunts me like an unyielding ghost. I have to turn away to hide my displeasure. Judy shows her teeth, making small talk with Raul, but there's no honor behind it. Not like Oliver. Her smile is all nerves. She'll be mountbatten pink, which is perfect for her. Though, I still think it's more like purple. Burlywood is still up for grabs.

Breakfast is day five of leaves. My stomach growls objections. The Collective's morning greetings are white noise against chirping crickets in the forest. Their music is something I love, but not as much as Becca. The mattress is thin in the guest cube. I hope her back aches with betrayal. When she emerges from the seafoam door, The Intern is with her, followed by Tammy, plum. His fingers strangle Tammy's hand. Three sets of eyes glitter with shared secrets. My rage is white hot flame. A fistful of leaves keeps my scream inside, cheeks so full the air barely reaches my lungs. Not enough oxygen to jump over the table. Definitely not enough to poke out their leering eyes. She can't do this much longer. It's the last day. She will have to face me.

It's her nature. I try to self-soothe.
Somewhere she loves me. I breathe again.
I know it.

Tammy catches my eyes before I can lift my mug to block her. She smiles and I smile back, awkward. She is coming my way, pulling The Intern behind her by his clammy fingers. It's too late to move.

"Morning, Gem."

How dare she smile and greet me like nothing's wrong? I smell Becca's desire on her breath. "Morning."

Becca sits beside The Intern, half an ass cheek wobbling off the wooden bench. She faces him and Tammy, like I'm a bit of fog, a memory, something forgotten.

"Do you all always eat leaves?" The Intern grabs a handful of them from his bowl, lets them cascade back inside one by one. "Not that they're not ... great." He rolls his eyes.

Becca pretends she doesn't notice the disrespect. "It's only for the ceremony. Actually, Tammy here is quite a good cook." They make eye contact. For far too long. Perhaps I hate Tammy, too.

"Oh stop." Tammy bats her bony shoulder.

I suck at my lukewarm coffee.

"So, what's next?" The Intern asks. "For the ceremony?"

"The dyeing starts tonight," I blurt, more to remind Becca than to inform him. *It's your last day.* I wonder if she can read my mind. She glances at me, but only for a moment.

Tammy's maroon hair is tangled in the back. Dyed. A shame. Before the dyeing, they will have to cut it off. Extra steps.

"Where do you keep the worms?" he asks. I've been waiting for this question.

"Worms?" I raise a brow.

Becca's cheeks flush.

Tammy's eyes wander away.

"The silkworms." His overly plucked brows furrow.

"Of course." The air is lighter. Becca and Tammy both remember to breathe it. I wouldn't mess it up for us. They should know that. Becca should know me better than that. "I'll show you tonight. If you'd like."

The Intern's greedy eyes eat up half the world. He wobbles his head like a wooden toy. I hate him.

Crisis averted, Tammy excuses herself to shower. "Scrub hard," I say. It's a tiny dig. One she well deserves.

The Intern slaps a hand onto Becca's thigh like he owns her. I see the spark in her amber irises. She is immune to ownership. Allergic. "Shall we ..." he trails off. Like she should know. As if they're some long married couple. She pulls away from him. I don't hide my smile. *I know you.* I try to think it hard enough so she might hear.

"Actually, I'd better head home for a bit," she says.

His shoulders fall. Smile fades. My insides dance with delight.

Crestfallen, he retreats to the guest cube. It's only she and I now. Her golden hair is greasy at her crown. She needs me to wash it.

"Burlywood is still up for grabs," I say. I want to scare her. Can't help it. Want her to fight for me.

She shrugs instead. "Maybe you should volunteer." Her clear words are a hiss.

"Maybe I will."

She shrugs again. "Maybe you should."

Becca saunters to our porch. Her hips sway in the passing breeze.

I am made of fire and hate.

There is something wrong with Becca.

***

Evening closes in around us and the gods paint the sky mountbatten pink. This is a sign. They have seen my lack of faith and I am naked before them, shivering.

It is not purple. I whisper my apology.

Hendricks returned to eat the peanuts. He left a bobby pin in their place. He loves me at least, and he forgives me. The gods shoot the sky through with vermillion as I fix the pins into my hair. Clouds bleed through the tree cover. Becca's outfit has laid on the bed for hours—an A-line dress, white silk and a sheer shawl to match, like a bride.

She taunts me.

I linger on the porch like I'm not allowed to see her. I know it's not real. It's not *our* Ceremony. I am not stupid. I know Becca can't love me. Not all the time.

The mice are hiding. They don't like what comes next, but know it must come, as do we all. The Intern paces with excitement, stammers about wishing he had his camera. He still doesn't understand. Cameras aren't allowed. No cars. No cameras. No phone. The Widow has been clear. The vats rest in a semicircle behind our picnic tables. Looms net us in from above, keep the birds away from the dye, though this is not their purpose. The Intern is talking about fashion now. About runway shows. About silk and satin and polyester blends. This is not the purpose. He still doesn't understand. "Can we go see the worms?"

I stare at him, wriggling. Imagine him coated in dirt.

He holds a small notebook in one hand, a pen in the other, and he jots down details.

"Yes, we're going now." From the porch I can look down at him, which seems right.

"It's for my paper," he says. "My professor will never believe it. I still can't believe—" He blushes. Men are stupid. "This is a once in a lifetime opportunity."

"It's every five years," I correct. I tower over him. Look down my nose. He ought to know.

The peach color about his stubbly cheeks turns scarlet. "Right, yeah. I know." His pen scrapes against the pad.

The Collective is gathering now, like ants trailing from their colorful shipping containers. They gather around the vats, all wondering the same thing. *Will we see The Widow?* I eye the rock face of Her natural stone home from the path. The Intern babbles behind me about threads and runway shows and I don't know what. I listen for trilling crickets, whose music I love, but they have gone quiet out of respect. The Widow is a homebody. I've not met Her yet in all these months. She sometimes leaves notes, elegant script formed on scrolls of treebark. Those days are so wonderful. She is like a mother to me. The vats await us. Plum, vermillion, mountbatten pink, burlywood, indigo. My very first ceremony.

Angela cleared fallen sticks and spider's webs from the overhead looms. They are ready and waiting to spin the threads. The Intern's voice is nails on porcelain, something about the worms again. Why doesn't he understand?

Becca will be late. I know this. She must always be a spectacle. I love her for it. Angela wears a cloak of many colors. It drags behind her in the dirt, despite its couture making and beauty. Nothing is too beautiful for the dirt. Her blonde hair has been dipped into the dyes. It gleams with every color of the Ceremony: indigo, vermillion, mountbatten pink, burlywood, plum. She bridges between the worlds.

"The Ceremony begins. We have waited many years for this moment. Prepared. I thank you all for your service and faith and sacrifice."

Oliver beams.

The color has gone from Judy's eyes.

The Intern waits to see the worms.

I glance over my shoulder for Becca. The light shows through our bedroom window. She is dressing.

"Our ancient ways bring the silk. The Widow feeds and spins the thread. The Collective weaves thread into cloth. The outsiders send us their money so the cycle may continue. We please the gods."

"Where is The Widow?" The Intern whispers.

I fold my arms. The gall of him. To expect after such little time to meet a god. "Don't worry. You will meet her."

"Where are the worms?"

I smirk.

Angela's voice is a roar. "I call upon our Intern, who has traveled far to witness this Ceremony. So few outsiders have the honor."

Tammy grasps his hand. I hadn't seen her in the crowd. She wears a navy cloak, hood pulled up, but I can still see her shaved head beneath its folds, nicked at her temple. She leads him to the vats. The lid is lifted off and The Intern stands beside it. Indigo dye so thick you can't see the bottom.

"It's tradition," Angela says.

Tammy grabs onto his shirt hem, lifts it up. Instinctively, he raises his arms, and she punishes us all with the sight of his naked, hairy chest and too-large nipples. She whispers into his ear, and he pulls down his pants and underwear. His pointed canines fall over his bottom lip.

The audacity of men.

"You honor us," Angela says as he swings one leg over the rim of the vat.

Tammy helps him inside and he slumps down so the dye is up to his chest. It's already joining with him, a pale cerulean tinge on his skin. He grins, still thinking of fashion and runways and worms.

When Raul and Oliver creep up from behind, The Intern doesn't notice—too impressed with his own sloshing and foolish grins. They lift the lid, and together bring it crashing down with such a force, that The Intern clunks against it and disappears like whack-a-mole. He struggles, legs beating against the metal sides.

Clunk, clunk, clunk, clunk.

I feel Becca behind me. I turn and see my bride. Her eyes are big as scrolls, her smile wider.

Clunk, clunk, clunk.

There is something wrong with Becca.

Clunk.

The rest of us, The Collective, we know this must be done.

Clunk, clunk.

For The Widow, for the gods. It is our honor.

Clunk, clunk, clunk, clunk.

But Becca ignites with joy at the sight of it, her shriveled heart made full.

Clunk, clunk, clunk. A bubbling groan.

I love her anyway. Not anyway. This is *why* I love her. She is more like The Widow than human, or maybe some other nasty god. She is beyond. I see her.

I see you, I mouth. Her smile changes. This one is only for me.

Clunk.

Oliver and Raul release their grip on the lid. I hear Judy breathing, a tiny whistle from her thin nose.

"It is finished," Angela says. "He is transformed." She gazes up at the sky, her cloak sliding down her shoulders. "Gods, with great honor, we present Indigo."

"For The Widow." It comes from all our mouths in unison.

There are no more clunks now, and the other vats are opened: vermilion, mountbatten pink, burlywood, and plum. It's a symphony of screeching metal and rustling cloaks as Judy, Tammy, and Oliver align in front. They stand beside their colors, soon to be one. Tammy and plum. Oliver and vermillion. Judy and mountbatten pink. I wave Becca over, but she resists me. Burlywood remains vacant.

"As always, we have saved one spot for a volunteer. This Ceremony's volunteer will have the great honor of becoming Burlywood. A fine, warm color." Angela scans the audience.

I look to Becca. She urges my hand into the air with her thick, shaped brows.

Betrayal. It's icy as it sinks in, from a jagged stone in my throat, to an anvil in my chest, to an emptiness in my gut. My raised palm casts long shadows across my face, hides me from the sinking sun.

"Gem! Wonderful."

There is clapping all around. It lifts me from my seat, carries me to the front with the others. When it rests, I'm beside Burlywood. Becca golf-claps behind the others, soundless.

"Now that you're all here," Angela lifts her hood over her rainbow hair, "we can begin. Our colors are as follows: Indigo is one taken. Mountbatten pink, plum, and vermillion are three assigned. Burlywood is one who volunteers. The quota is met."

The gods smile at me from above, so why does my heart not rejoice? I look to Becca instead, wait for her to intervene. She is still as death.

Angela drones on and her words make me pull off my shirt, slide my pants down around my hips. I feel them around my ankles, and I step out of them. There's a stickiness about my thighs. Sweat, I think, and I'm ashamed. If the others knew I'd forsaken my honor…

Becca points.

Angela pulls in a sharp breath. "We will need another volunteer."

My stomach turns over. They know I am afraid. They reject my sacrifice. I am made of revulsion and shame.

Raul crosses the dirt ground, picks up my pile of crumpled clothes. Clumsy, I pull on my shirt, bend down to stick my leg through the pants and—

Red smears stain my thighs. Congealed blood. I pull my pants on quickly. My heartbeat steadies. It was not shame they saw. They could not let me ruin the dye.

Becca has moved closer, circled her way to the picnic tables like a snake. She takes a seat in the center as Angela calls on the others for their willingness. I am proud to have offered. I take my seat beside her. Her hand is heavy and warm on my thigh.

"You knew?" I whisper as Petah volunteers to take my place.

She turns her hand to show me her palm, two fingers caked with blood. I lace mine into hers. This is the work of the gods. We are wedded now, in their eyes. They wish us to live, partnered.

I don't have to say it. Becca doesn't breathe a word. She squeezes my palm and Judy climbs inside mountbatten pink. She dunks her head beneath the surface and Angela sits atop the lid. She bangs and clangs inside. Fights her purpose. There are at least twenty *clunks*. It is a great shame.

Tammy holds her breath before going under plum. I'm embarrassed for her. She's quiet for a while, but *clunks* at least ten times before becoming Plum.

Oliver does much better. I knew he would. Only three small *clunks* at the end. I'm sure he couldn't help it. It's human nature. I swell with pride.

When Petah climbs inside I am looking into Becca's eyes. She is looking into mine. *You love me?* I ask with my blinks.

I've always loved you, she replies with the cadence of her breath.

The colors must sit overnight to fulfill their purpose, so the remaining Collective members scatter to their homes. Becca holds my hand the whole way. Passing lizards bob their heads in approval, wave their glorious throats at us like flags. Extra daisies have bloomed because they're happy for us.

***

The rising sun shakes me from my bed. I am a child again on Christmas morning. I shake Becca, and her eyes flutter as she remembers me.

"Do you think She will come?"

Becca leans toward me, plants gentle kisses on my eyelids. We are one. The gods have made it so. From our window I can squint to see through oak branches. The vats stand open, lidless.

"Becca!"

My bride rushes to join me. "She's come."

She drags me from the house, in no more than my long t-shirt. I barely think of Hendricks as our bare feet kick up loamy soil in our wake. We reach the picnic tables while the rest of The Collective still sleeps. Each vat holds remnants of spent dye. Becca tugs at my arm. My eyes follow her tilted chin to the looms overhead. Blankets of silk fiber drape over suspended netting around the looms. Brilliant swaths of Indigo, Plum, Burlywood, Mountbatten Pink, and Vermillion rest between branches. Squirrels, birds, and beetles stay away. They know better than to interfere.

"It's incredible."

The kaleidoscope of colors entrances me until I'm dizzy.

"We have spinning to do," I tell her.

"Wait, She's got to be around here somewhere."

Becca is curious. Too curious. She yanks my arm so hard it aches in the socket, and I follow her toward The Widow's stone home. Errant sticks dig into my soles. This path is not well worn. At the cave's entrance, we find the bones. They are stacked, tall intricate patterns so beautiful it makes my eyes hurt. Becca reaches out to touch them.

"Don't."

She touches them anyway, and the fragile structure quakes. I am made of fascination and fear. Becca takes quick steps back. There's a scratching from inside The Widow's home, like sticks or cartilage against rock. I strain my eyes against the darkness inside. A wing beat. Becca is a statue beside me. There's a flutter in the dark, a flash of white. A feathered antenna, taller than Becca or I. The rustling makes me reach my hand into the black. My fingertips tremble. I wait for death, but instead find pillowy smoothness against my flesh.

"Is She—-"

I reach my other hand back to shush Becca.

Of course. The Widow is our mother. We are the worms.

Today we will spin the silk into threads, and Becca will love me. Tomorrow she may not, but still, I'll spin the silk. That is her nature, and this is mine.

There is something wrong with Becca.

But we are bound together now. Bound by gods and the moon and a mile of silken thread.

Common Oleander

Published by Samantha Kolesnik in *Moonflowers and Nightshade*, September 2022

Oleander reigns the undisputed queen of the garden. Her five-fingered pink blossoms sprawl above the white tufts of flowering water hemlock and his cousin, white snakeroot. *Not cousin*, Becca always reminds me, but I am more vulnerable to aesthetics and less interested in genus and species. I prefer to think of them as not-so-distant relations, parted for many years and now reunited, here in our yard.

I watch Becca. She's sitting cross-legged, leaves swaying on sprawling stems about her cheeks. Breezes entangle them in her natural blonde hair, which flows freely. She prunes by hand.

I used to worry. When she saw my wide eyes the first time I caught her pinching off yellow leaves with her fingernails, she giggled.

"Isn't that—"

"You have to eat it, sweetie," she'd said.

Now we pass the morning hours here. I, with my steaming tea in the wicker chair, and she, still in her nightgown, barefoot amidst her flora. This is our spring routine.

"Castor bean's unhappy," she says. Her mouth tightens and my guts twitch. "You'll run into town, won't you? Pick up some bananas for the PH?"

"Of course." I sigh. An easy fix. When the spider mites came last year, it wasn't so simple. I spent weeks tiptoeing around her volatile mood.

"And don't let Betsy see you." A given. She plucks seeds from the castor bean. Dirt has blackened the soles of her feet. "When will our visitor arrive?"

"Soon."

Rolling hills surround us on all sides, dotted by off-white cottages so much like our own. Most of the neighbors prefer their views unrestricted, but our five acres are bordered by a simple wooden post fence. It's not enough to keep the foxes from wandering in, or the stray dogs. In fact, it's mostly ceremonial, but the twists of barbed wire around the entry tell the odd salesman or religious zealot, *you are most unwelcome*. And for us, that is enough.

Uncut grasses sway over the landscape, an ocean of billowing green. My eyes scan the horizon, trace our simple fence, return to Becca, then follow the garden to its limit, where the freshly dug soil wriggles with earthworms. Seeds in hand, she takes her seat beside me, wicker threads bending with her weight. Unfurling her palm, she lifts them to my face for inspection.

"Despite the rich burgundy leaves, castor seeds are cool tone brown, specked in heterogeneous patterns." She points one out. "This one's spotted like a leopard."

This close, I can smell her intoxicating mix of lavender soap and organic earth.

"Looks like a beetle to me."

She smirks, and her amber eyes meet mine. Smoothing back a wisp of my hair, her finger traces my earlobe. "Gem—"

My insides collapse. She knows my name on her lips makes me swoon.

"Let's just sit here a while."

Blood rushes to my cheeks.

"At least until our guest arrives."

Five years together and still I find myself completely disarmed by her. Woefully enchanted. "Of course, baby." I lean in, as she knew I would, and her eyes gently close, her chin tilting upward. My lips sink into her supple kiss. Her tongue skims the ridges of my teeth, and I'm lost until she pulls away.

"Can I see it?"

Her brow arches, and I take her by the hand. Through the living web of bushes and vines, she trails me. Our small shed doesn't hold much: the wheelbarrow, spare hose, seedling trays, and it needs another coat of periwinkle paint, but inside I show her I'm prepared. Bags of woodchips and sawdust piled atop one another earn me a beaming grin and the feeling of her arms around my waist.

"The nitrogen mixes with the carbon and makes a happy home for microbes," she begins to explain again, holding me tight.

"I know. I remember."

The distant sputtering of an engine draws our attention to the one-lane road.

"Is that him?" she asks, as if I could know for sure.

Muted red, the truck rises above a hilltop then slopes back down, out of sight. It winds through the gentle curves, the melody of a country song riding in on a breeze as it draws closer.

"Go put the tea on," she says.

By the time he knocks, the water has warmed, and Becca has stepped into the shower. I remove the kettle from the burner, and twirl the spiraling steam. I let him loiter on the porch until he knocks a second time. I spy through the peephole. He's a few years older than he said, his dark hair shot through with gray. It must have been an old picture. He shifts his weight, taps on his jeans and rubs his palm over a tear in the denim.

"Who is it?" I ask through the door.

His eyes roll. "Paul. Paul Richards? Aren't you expecting me?" Hairline wrinkles form between his unkempt brows.

"Paul Richards?" I pretend to confirm. I understand using a false name, but he could've put a bit more thought into his pseudonym.

"Maybe I have the wrong—"

I open the door. His tank top looks even more faded and pitiful without the peephole's distortion.

"I'm here about the groundskeeper position." He scratches at his belly where it bulges over his pants. "Do I have the wrong house?"

Not in the way you mean. "Of course." I put on my hostess smile. "Come on in, I've just made a pot of tea."

I usher him to the couch where he wavers before he sits, as if sitting on the rose pattern might somehow diminish his masculinity. Pouring us each a cup of tea, I settle in the loveseat. Vapors from my cup waft around my nose and I take in the floral scent. He gulps his down in two swallows.

"I've forgotten the trail mix! You must think I'm a lousy host." I nestle my cup on its matching saucer and return to the kitchen, feeling his impatience on my back. On his lap I place a bowl of pretzels, candies, nuts, and other goodies. He tosses a handful into his irritated grimace.

"It's all cash, right?" he says through chomps, peppering the air with bits of chewed nuts.

"That's right."

The water turns off.

"Becca will be with us in just a moment."

"Who?"

"She likes to be part of the interviews."

He nods and leans back against the sofa cushions. His legs spread, knees squaring with his shoulders now that he's comfortable. Becca calls them guests or visitors, but I think of them as candidates. They are, after all, here to fill a vacant role. I've found through experience that offering cash brings in a particular type of man, the type with reasons not to use his real name. Becca doesn't get hung up on these sorts of things. She's all about results. But I prefer it this way.

"Do you live in town?" I ask, though I know the answer.

"Yeah," he lies. "Not far."

I nod. In a town of four hundred, it's easy to know when you're talking to an outsider. He pulls his phone from his pocket, the flip kind. I guess I'm boring him.

"Is it nostalgia?" Becca asks, parading out of the bedroom. She's put on a sundress, vivid yellow pansies against white cotton.

Our candidate sports a puzzled look. Not an ironic hipster then.

"Follow me to the garden." Becca takes long strides out the French doors. Her speed lifts the hem of her dress, giving a tantalizing view of her upper thigh. I watch him stare. She talks maintenance work, but his eyes focus on her lips. I stand beside her, and rub her shoulder while she speaks.

"You two sisters?" he asks.

I don't try to hide the pang of anger. In a larger city, I think my short hairstyle would offer a clue. But here in the Meadowland it's just as common on the hetero farmers' wives.

"This is common oleander," she explains, drifting from my side and gazing at the pink blossoms like a paramour. "But I think you'll agree there's nothing common about mine."

He steps between Becca and me.

Her hand hovers over the delicate petals. "You must never touch them. The sap can cause rashes for some people. Not me." She plucks a single bloom, tucks it behind her ear.

"What's this one," he asks, feigning interest as he motions toward the wide leaves of our tobacco patch.

"That one you can touch." *Touch* pulls her mouth into a seductive O shape.

Beads of sweat form at his hairline. I sit in my wicker chair.

"Funny thing about tobacco. Even children know that smoking it will kill you, but far less know that the faster death comes if you eat the leaves."

He glances over, sizing me up, letting her words fall into the background.

"And this one," she goes on, "rosary pea. People make jewelry from the seeds, which are perfectly harmless intact."

A droplet rolls down his temple. He bites at his cheek.

"But they contain abrin. So any jewelry makers with pricked fingers and cracked seeds have a painful few days of organ failure before their death."

He snorts. "Lucky for me, I don't make jewelry."

She nods. "I'm sure you know about castor bean."

"Can't say I do."

"It only takes two seeds to kill a child. More for an adult."

His hand clutches at his stomach. I hear it grumble and flip from twenty feet away.

"How much trail mix did you say you ate?"

He retches, and his skin turns a shade of gray. Stumbling off the path, he dry heaves.

"White snakeroot killed Lincoln's mother. And water hemlock, believe it or not, is in the carrot family."

Both hands clutch at his abdomen. His shoulders quake.

"People sometimes confuse it with celery or parsnips. But considering the cicutoxin, it's the last mistake they tend to make."

He stumbles to his knees. She points around the garden, one plant at a time.

"Cicutoxin, atropine and scopolamine, tremetol, ricin—I'm sure you've heard of that one—abrin, anabasine," she floats back to the queen—precious oleander. "And oleandrin, of course."

Thick vomit pours from his mouth. It collects on his chin in chunks.

"You didn't get that one though. I couldn't bear to sacrifice even a cutting of it. Not this close to the festival."

The realization comes to him, and his surprise mixes with rage. He crawls toward her, lashing out with wild hands. She steps backward, easily avoiding his flailing limbs.

"Vomiting, diarrhea, convulsions. Most of the toxins have a similar effect, which I'm sure you can attest to."

A seizure rocks his body. Thin foam drizzles from his mouth.

"Shouldn't be long now."

A gurgling groan emits from his throat as he makes his last stand. To my shock, he regains his footing, and I see my own fear reflected in Becca's eyes. He catches hold of her and I dash around the side of the house to grab our rusty shovel. Tiny splinters wedge into my unprotected palms as I dig my fingernails into the wooden handle for grip. When I clear the corner, he's taken her to the ground, punching wildly about her head.

Bone cracks as the metal spade makes contact, and Becca rolls his stunned body off hers. She staggers to her feet, and I bring the shovel down over his bleeding head again and again, unwilling to take any chances. His skull reduced to pulpy fragments, I toss the tool aside. Becca takes her place by my side, and a few drops of blood spill from her nose.

"What a shame."

My heart skips at the sound of Betsy's voice. Becca goes pale. We both turn toward the north end of the property, and there she is, leaning on the fence post, peering at us beneath the wide brim of her church hat.

Becca wipes her nose with the back of her arm, leaving a streak of burnt orange on her upper lip.

Betsy motions toward the garden and we see it. Broken stems, fallen flowers, scattered leaves. A man-sized indent where his tackle flattened the nightshade patch. Becca falls to her knees. Her eyes water as the battered stems drape limply around her grasp.

"Looks like you'll have to start over from seeds." There's a smug quality to her tone.

I retort. "Unfortunately for you, the oleander is untouched."

Betsy crinkles her nose. "No matter. My champion blooms speak for themselves every year at the festival. This year will be no different."

Becca dusts off her knees and sulks inside, mourning the loss of her brood.

"Go tend to them, then," I insist.

She smirks. "I shall." Sneaking one last glance at the candidate's broken body, she adds, "You'd better get going anyhow. You've got your work cut out for you today I see."

Plodding away through the long grasses, she leaves a depressed trail of folded stalks in her wake. Despite my disdain for her, I know she's right. Disarticulating his body will consume me through nightfall. I know better than to try to comfort Becca. She is, no doubt, back under the scalding shower, calculating the time it will take to regrow her nightshade to the fullness and luster of the decimated patch.

I spend hours stripping away the flesh, unwinding the tendons, and sawing through bones. Clotted blood soaks into the earth and it saturates the ground. I've finally got him into manageable pieces. I relocate his hands, disconnected at the wrist—his shins, detached at the knee and ankle—and feet, to perfectly-sized holes around the garden. I lay his pieces atop woodchips and sawdust, and cover them up with thick layers of soil. The largest hole is reserved for the torso, so heavy I have to drag it. Becca doesn't help with this part. She never does. We each have our role, our spring routine. When he's firmly planted, the sun is dipping beneath the horizon, staining the green hills orange. I return to the house, a collection of wildflowers in hand. It's a small offering to soothe Becca's loss. Wordlessly, she puts them in water.

"Is it true, you think?" Her lip quivers.

My arm circles her hips. I lead her to the couch, and she settles beside me.

"Betsy may have a winning streak, but she was supplementing long before we moved here. We've got to give it time."

Becca shakes her head, and stares at the seam where the wall meets the hardwood. "It's the realtor's fault. He should've mentioned the loamy soil. If we'd have known—"

I pull her into my embrace before she can spiral. It's easier to blame. Even if we didn't garden then or know about the Meadowland Festival.

"The Hendricks are judging this year. Betsy knows they haven't liked her since the incident with the goats. She came over here to taunt us just to boost her fragile ego, old coot."

Becca sniffs and composes herself with fragile hope. "Do you really think we have a shot?"

I gaze into the depths of her amber eyes. "Your oleanders are stunning, my love. World class. And by May, our visitor will be feeding them, boosting their luscious bouquets. I wouldn't be surprised if we got magenta hues."

I weave my fingers into the waves of her hair. Her soft breath warms my chest. Tomorrow I'll make tea. Becca will wander barefoot into the garden and prune bushes by hand in her nightgown. I'll watch from my wicker chair.

This is our spring routine.

Of Ash and Soot

Published by Eerie River Publishing in *Fire*,
November 2022

The sky is sickly gray, but not with cloud cover. Sunlight leaks through the hanging smoke, the color of gasoline. This is a good day. And there have been so few since the fires. Ten feet ahead, Becca crumbles char beneath her bare feet. She hops from lump to lump, giggling like a child skipping puddles. Her blonde locks stained, her pale skin coated in snowflake ash, she is like some awoken creature, clawed up from deep earth.

"Isn't it wonderful?" Arms outstretched, eyes to the putrid sky, she spins slow.

I cannot help but love her.

My pulse quickens as I glance behind. "We should get back." The roads are not safe now, too many survivors left behind. But still Becca spins. From the shop at my side, I hear glass shards clink and rustle. Hot blood rushes to my hands and my ears ring as I turn to the shattered picture window. Becca doesn't notice. No doubt the whooshing of passing wind drowns the sound. My shoulders stiffen. I assume my predator form. Eyes passing over the scattered hats inside: derbys, bowlers, fedoras. The scent of ironic hipsters mixes with the toxic fumes of melted chemicals I can't pronounce. I brace for impact as I move closer.

Below eye level, a whir of color. A voice, no, a coo penetrates the fetid air. My need for violence dissipates as I see her. Tiny, shivering, a child pushes a wide brimmed hat across the floor. Her face is scrunched, her ashy hair pushed into odd angles. She looks upon me as a mother, and my heart sinks. I don't think any mothers survived.

"Hello," I say in my kindest voice.

Her too big eyes meet mine, a plea.

Becca is beside me now. She crouches. "And who do we have here?"

Cold settles in my gut.

Becca steps between the remnants of the window, her bare feet wise with instinct. When she reaches her hands toward the girl, it is as if they are icy, wrapped around my throat. But to my relief, she lifts her, holds her close to her chest. She bounces up and down, gentle as a rocking horse.

"What's your name?" she asks.

The girl's eyes fill to the brim, and I think she might wail.

"We should go," I say. "If she cries—"

"Would you like to come with us, little sparrow?" Becca keeps bouncing, a bit too hard now. The girl's head jostles.

Clopping of hooves against asphalt spurs us both into action. They are coming, and we have no choice but to run. Our feet carry us onward. We know the way. Through the back alleys littered with unpaired shoes and abandoned weapons, to the dirt road, to the boat launch where we follow the footpath into the swamp. Muck slows our steps, latching onto our feet with sucking sounds. Sawgrass knicks at our thighs, but still we run. We follow the trail to where our own smoke rises, from the tiny campfire we call our own.

The others, Linda and Ron, brew stale coffee in a pot suspended over the fire. This is a good, kind place, except for the mosquitoes. Becca places the girl down on the overturned log beside the fire. She eyes our pitched tents with hopes of a home.

"Look what I found," Becca says, proud.

I see the whites of Ron and Linda's eyes as they consider what to make of this. There are no mothers left.

"It will be so fun." Becca's voice is high and bounces off our tent poles. "Be right back!"

She disappears into the thick marsh.

"What will we…" I say it as a whisper. Becca's steps are close enough to hear.

"She can't stay." Linda's voice is hoarse. She inhaled too much smoke when it happened. Rob's lips are a tight line.

"I'm back!" Becca launches through blades of grass taller than any of us, her fists filled with lily pad flowers. The girl is slumped over on the log. She looks weak. She looks tired.

Becca hands a flower to the girl, who inspects it and touches it to her tongue. Slender fingers wind through the girl's hair, lacing flower stems between the strands. "You're going to look like a princess," she says.

The girl takes a cautious bite of a petal before Becca snatches it away.

"I think she's hungry," Linda says.

"I'll heat up some beans," Rob offers.

Becca's smile contorts into a scowl.

"It's beautiful," I say, but she's unimpressed with my faint praise and storms into our tent.

The day is a flurry of hesitant efforts at care. Offerings of beans. Towel baths of mucky swamp water. Tying the girl's shirt where it's ripped in the back. Becca resigns herself to discontented sleep, and when I settle in for the night, she is waking like some nocturnal animal. The moonlight paints her silver as she sits over the sleeping girl beside the fire.

"I'll watch her," she says. "Wouldn't want her wandering off..." But there's no mothering in her eyes when she says it, and her eyes reflect the cold indifference of the waxing moon.

I zip the tent door and try to picture Becca as a mother. She is many things, this woman I love: feral, bewitching, at times, hysterical. She wants to burn the world to the ground, and she tried. But at the edges of my spirit lingers a hope. This could be the thing to change her. To settle the gaping hole inside. *Yes, perhaps it will mend her,* I think as I drift into sleep. The thought of it comforts me, and I disappear into the white noise of bullfrogs and crickets playing tiny violins.

***

I wake with a start the next morning and throw open the flap separating Becca from me. Only the smoldering fire sits in the center of camp. I jump to my feet. Linda and Rob's silhouettes twitch and rollover inside their tent. Still sleeping. So, I follow the folded reeds, angry brush striking at my feet as I wade into the marsh. Water rises, or I descend, until it licks at my hips. I reach a clearing where I spot them, and my pulse rests for a moment, until I see the beady eyes over the water's surface, the ridges of its reptilian back, and tiny, dangling feet just above.

"Becca!" I yell. She snaps the girl close to her body. The gator hovers just a few feet away. "What the hell are you doing?"

Becca smiles as if she can fool me, and tiptoes along the bank, child in hand, until she reaches my side. "Thought she'd like to meet a gator, that's all."

I extend my arms and she surrenders the child to me. She's weighty, perhaps two or three. I push a bit of muck from beneath her eye.

"Let's get back to camp." I shudder at the thought of the girl slipping from Becca's arms, breaking the water's surface with a *clunk*. Surely she didn't intend to... but she might've. Spontaneously I remember an obscure fact from grade school, *alligators hunt at dawn and at dusk.* I push the thought from my mind.

When we return, Linda and Rob are heating oatmeal over the fire in their all-purpose pot. A thin layer of ash coats the lid like fresh snow. The girl pushes against my body and leans toward the sugary smell. She is hungry. We are all hungry.

The day is humid and hot and still. Linda languishes in her tent, her sputtering coughs a steady reminder of the slow death we all breathe.

"We're almost out of firewood," Becca says, tossing the last dry branch onto the flames. Embers rise like fireflies and circle the air inches from the girl's face. She wrenches her head back and swats at them. "I'll go into the hammock."

I nod. It is understood that I'll follow her. The girl tottles behind us until we reach the deeper water, where I let her cling to my back, though she tears the collar of my shirt. The hardwood hammock rises from the marsh like an old god. Cyprus knees make the climb ashore difficult, and the clinging toddler more so, but I pull myself up from the muck, child in tow and lay amongst the brambles. I huff and catch my breath from the slog.

"If you're tired, maybe you should leave it here." Becca wipes at her face, clearing streaks of soot beneath her eyes and leaving streaks of clean skin like warpaint. Her hair curls with moisture and warmth, and I find it odd that someone so lovely could be so full of sticky nothingness. She searches for dry wood while I watch the girl entertain herself with a fluffy cattail. I hear Becca's step circle the small island, double back, and circle again.

"I don't know if there's anything left to burn," I say.

I startle when her voice is so close. "There is always something else to burn." It's a hiss. A threat. I grab the girl's chubby hand out of instinct. Becca towers over her.

"You think you're special or something?" She stoops down, her vacant eyes meeting the girl's too big ones. "Just because you don't have parents?"

The girl's lip trembles. I hope she doesn't understand.

"You are not so special." Becca spits into the muck, and I gather the girl into my arms.

I have to change the subject, refocus Becca. "We'll have to go into town again."

Becca *hmphs* in agreement.

The walk to town is slow going. Becca leads by fifty feet or more, refusing to slack her pace. I carry the girl when I can, and when the heat makes my vision swirl, I lead her by her plump, fragile arm. I plan to leave her. Maybe the men on horses can take her. Maybe she'll be safer with them. Maybe they know of a mother.

When we reach the old mill, Becca stacks 2x4s into a pile, discarding the ones that are too charred. I think of how I miss the sun and wonder whether the girl will remember the shine of a sun unobstructed.

"I thought I saw some canned goods down the road yesterday, when we were running." I hope she'll believe the lie.

She doesn't face me when she answers, "Well, what're you waiting for then?"

I release an anxious breath. This is my chance. The sound of wood banging against wood grows distant as I move down the torched street. Cars with windows busted out from the heat line the road, miscellaneous papers flutter through a stagnant breeze. The whole town is choked, life burned away. I put the girl on my back and turn a corner, and my heart drops through simmering asphalt as my eyes are met with a big brown pair.

A woman, cloaked in navy fabric, stares back at me. Her jaw hangs open, her palms open. No weapon. I show her my empty hands. "It's okay," I whisper. I lower the child and place her on her tiny feet between us. "Are you a mother?"

The woman says nothing, mouth still agape.

"Please, you have to take her." I take a careful step away. The girl looks to me then to the new woman. "You have to go with her, okay?" I take another step back.

The woman's wide eyes flash to something behind me, and I turn, though I already know what I'll see.

Becca has followed me. Of course. She stands some ten feet away, a plank of wood in her hand, jagged nails jutting out from the board. She has the stance of a warrior and wears her black, deep hunting eyes.

I inhale with every intent of begging Becca to stop, but the woman has already grabbed the child and started running. My words die in my throat as I watch Becca take off after them, swinging the vicious board over her head and screaming like a banshee.

"Becca!" I yell, or I think I yell, but perhaps it's just in my head. I follow but she's quick as a panther, the woman and child just steps ahead. Rusty stains appear beneath Becca's feet, and sparkling shards of glass are cast out behind her like stones. She cries out. It's pain, it's anguish, it's trauma. She stops running, whips the board away. Teeth bared, she emits a guttural scream. She is living rage. Her chest rises and falls like a beating heart as the woman and child are absorbed by thick overgrowth.

I catch up to her, panting. I feel her fear, her torment. I wrap my arm around Becca as a child. Her words are soft as molten lead.

"I hope they don't make it."

I reach down and lace my fingers through hers. "I know."

Her eyes fill with tears. "I hope none of us do."

I guide her, like I did the child, out of the road. Like I am a mother. We both stare into the place where they disappeared. I remember what she said when this all started. Her words carry over a melody in my mind. *On every pile of ash there is a woman dancing, or screaming, or fighting for her life. And who can tell the difference?*

Gemma Prepared to Dive

Package to Sandra Harraway, contents including:
The journal of Gemma Roberts
A letter from Mallory Daines

The Journal of Gemma Roberts
September 2nd

Weeks since I've seen the crisp smile of blank parchment, it's with great delight I return to you, dear journal. The men back home made no exaggeration on the dangers of the sea. I fear I'll never forget the crooning of whalers as they clung to their ship, tipped entirely to one side like a lame cow. Brendon called it a *knock down*, and when I pleaded to rescue the men, assured me it happens quite often, that the whalers are accustomed to righting the vessel and wait only for the proper angle of a passing wave. My fretfulness over their fate was, in truth, a welcome distraction from my impending arrival. But having met port last night, I can no longer pretend. Becca is here, somewhere, and I shall find her.

I'm not so easily pushed off course by tall tales, despite Sandra's best efforts. The island's residents cannot be all they say. I feel quite steadied by the thought that–more likely than any of the monstrous attributions cruelly bestowed upon them by town gossips and drunken men, bittered by their inability to sail in old age–those of Bell Harbor are simply an isolated people. Insular. Contented with their own customs and leading lives quite as joyful and fulfilling as those of city-dwellers. How seriously can one take the word of sea-faring men?

Not very.

I myself have painfully nodded through myriad recounts of adventures more fantasy than fishing.

So no, I do not fear the village or its villagers therein. What I fear, the deep serpent circling my ship, is that I shall indeed find Becca, only to be rejected by her once more. My lids grow heavy and the candle's wick grows short. Tomorrow I depart from the inn and find my way to Bell Harbor. I shall write again in the evening. Sleep well, journal.

September 3rd

Well, journal, the day was long and the journey difficult. I suppose, against sense, I expected a cabbie similar to what I might find back home, one who would trudge my baggage along. Of course, I did not find one, and began my day's trip dragging my trunk inch by inch against the harsh chorus of the driver repeating, *Last call! Last call to Bell!*

Any semblance of grace in my hairstyle was long gone by the time I climbed inside the coach, curls frizzed with humidity and rouge streaked through from beads of sweat. Bearing none of the luxury of transport one might find in a city such as New York, the coach was not altogether objectionable. Wooden seats were softened with a slim (if not lumpy) cushion. As I said, not luxury, but I could not altogether complain. The ride was a fascinating one. Never have I seen such fauna and flora as reside here. I spent hours quite content, staring at passing magenta blossoms, even caught a glimpse of a rat-like creature, though it was long and drawn out as if stretched, and its large black eyes were more welcoming than beady. For all the trepidation around speaking of Bell Harbor, thus far, I find it lovely.

About halfway through our drive, I asked the cabbie about Becca, whether he knew her (to which he responded with a curt shake of the head), then whether he'd heard of her (to which he paused, twisted his lips, then grunted). I inquired after the meaning of the grunt, small hope fluttering within my gut, but he took to ignoring me, perhaps miffed that I'd not yet tipped him for hoisting my trunk into the carriage. Journal, it was the least he could do, my brow soaked with sweat as it had been and him having watched me wrestle the damned thing from room to road. Needless to say, we completed the remainder of our ride in quiet.

I'd scarcely believed Sandra when she'd said there were no inns at Bell but felt an overwhelming gratitude upon my arrival when I discovered how right she was. Thankfully, she'd corresponded with some locals who, after some hesitation, agreed to host me in a spare bedroom. While less than ideal, had the preparation not been made I would find myself writing beside the flickering glow of a campfire tonight as sprinkles of rain wet your pages.

My host is a rather rotund woman with a leery eye, reddened cheeks. and gray streaked hair. From the sparseness of her small home, I'd guess she lives a frugal, pragmatic life. She too did nothing to aid as I struggled with my trunk, merely pointed in the direction of the room which was to be mine.

"Thank you," I'd said, feeling rather self-conscious in the wake of the somewhat tepid greeting. "I'll get this settled and be glad for a tour." Upon reflection, journal, I wonder whether she would've offered a tour at all had I not mentioned one. In any case, it was short. Her living room walls were mostly bare, one rusted spear hung (slightly crooked) on the peeling and faded floral paper. The couch coughed up a fine cloud of dust when I sat upon it, but I did my best not to let on that I'd noticed. After all, as I said, it was either her home or moist soil and a campfire.

It was, perhaps, the absence of decor which drew my attention to the small token upon the kitchen counter: a twisting, curling shape I could not easily identify carved from a slick, black material. It seemed to me the only thing untouched by a layer of film. I thought better of asking about it, finding myself unable to articulate an appropriate comment on the thing. To say it was beautiful would've been dishonest, and to call it *interesting* may have sounded critical. So I said nothing, which seemed to suit her quite well.

"Mallory," she said. And I took it to be her name. "My husband should be back tomorrow."

A slight nod from me and she went to the main bedroom, closing the door behind her. I cannot help but feel it was a bit of rudeness; however, if I'm transparent, I admit that I'm fatigued and would just as soon spend the evening in solitude. Tomorrow I shall ask Mallory about Becca. I know she is here. Having wiped a clean circle in the small window, I have a partial view of the dense forest growth. And journal, though it might sound mad, even the smooth curvature of the vines remind me of her. The song of those bluish birds must be the same key in which she once hummed. I feel her here, and I will find her.

I will make it right.

September 4th

Timothy Daines returned before dawn with a racket, taking no care in stacking crab traps at the side of the house beneath my window. The clock on the bureau read half past five, and I made the determination to dress and ready myself. And good thing, for Tim (in rather a brooding manner) insisted I accompany them to church. Unsure what to wear, I selected a patterned dress with a hem well below my knees, thinking of modesty. I was embarrassed to find its shade of yellow clashed with Mallory's, hers faded and pilled from too many rough washings, but to change again would invite a scene.

The morning service was unlike any I've attended in the city, but it offered an excellent chance to mingle with the locals and take stock of them. It seems Mallory and Tim's coldness is a quality shared by all people here. I caught a few wandering eyes assessing me, an obvious outsider in the dim room, and a too-yellow speck amongst the usual parishioners. Though few words were said, and even fewer introductions made, I figure stoicism to be a norm in Bell, and thus am doing my best not to take it personally.

I managed to catch a boy on his way to the washroom and ask him whether he knew Becca. His light eyes gaped, his body went rigid, and for a moment I thought he might turn and run. To my relief, he did no such thing, just took a steadying breath and invited me back to services on Wednesday evening. It was a strange encounter, journal. One I do not wish to repeat. Between that and the sour moods of my hosts, I've resolved to scout out Becca by other means. I'll attend the services, explore the docks and whatever shops might run in the small town center, but I'll not ask after her with the locals. They seem averse to conversation, and I worry if I pry with an adult, I might find myself unwelcome here.

It is nearly midday. If I start walking now, I believe I can make it to the meat market and bakery and back before sundown. I trust you'll hold my mission in confidence, journal, and look forward to writing again soon.

September 4th (Evening)

I returned to find a book upon my bed. Bound in black leather and inscribed with gold lettering, it appears well-loved, pages softened with time and reading. I searched for

Mallory to thank her but found both she and Tim must have busied themselves with some errand or another.

While the trip to town relinquished no sign of Becca, I find no temptation to dwell on this small failure, for within the text of this gifted book are most intriguing sketches and prose. I'll not jump to assumptions, journal. I'll wait until I've given it more than a cursory glance to say more, but I wonder whether it might hold some secret to the island. And if so, perhaps some clue as to the whereabouts of Becca. They are an unusual pair, Mallory and Tim. I was struck by their coldness upon my arrival and am now struck again by the seemingly warm gesture of a gift. It all shows that I have much yet to learn: about my hosts and about the island if I've any real chance of a reunion with my lost love.

September 6th

I first must apologize for my absence, but oh the comings since I last wrote! It took the better part of the day to complete the book but was well worth the investment of time. I now understand the origin of the tall tales spewed about this place. Their lore is most provocative! My initial impulse, when reading of the water women within its pages, of their seductive nature and equally violent delights, was to slam the cover shut, put it away, and think of it no more. But that should make me a hypocrite, journal. For we both know well my interest in the feminine form, and how it has always held me just outside of "decent" society. I am filled with so many things! Struck by the mythos and equally intrigued by the reverence attributed to these entities. If the villagers believe this lore, might they accept a love like mine and Becca's? Do they believe them, journal? Or is it mere story?

No, it cannot be. Such loving detail was bestowed upon the water women, from their glowing eyes to the greenish hue of their lustrous hair. They speak of power untold, ancient rites, and ethereal balance. People who share stories such as this must not share the prudish beliefs of those in the cities. And so, it makes logical sense that Bell Harbor would be villainized as it is. Even Sandra would think the villagers to be *radicals*.

Let me slow down, for I race ahead of my own thoughts.

The book tells of a hidden, bottomless cove where the water is not brackish or salt, but pure, the purest and clearest water one might ever find. Within these waters, it is said, dwells the water women–angry, vengeful spirits. But they are no mere ghosts! No, they are the souls of the drowned, the abused, the downtrodden. And while they seek to harm, they seek also to give. Chapters upon chapters are devoted to rites and offerings to the water women. Rites that bring forth blessed harvests (though I cannot imagine what could be harvested in soil such as this), bountiful fishing, and even fertility. It is said that by honoring them, the water women tend to the *great void*. I must confess, I've been unable to discern what exactly is meant by this *void*, but my best understanding is that it represents everyday horrors–disease, avarice, famine.

So fascinated I was by my reading, I sought out Mallory to speak with her, and to thank her, but she said only to join them in service on Wednesday. Of course, I intend to. But how I yearn to wander, journal. I wonder whether I might find the cove if I should look. I'd hate to be lost to the thick jungle, but what if Becca dwells there? Drawn to women as she is, I would think such a place would appeal to her greatly. Yes, the more and more I think, the more I am convinced this is where I will find her. And find her, I must. For the *great void* is already upon me, and ever has been since she left. It threatens to swallow me whole should I not escape from its clutches.

It is decided. You convince me, journal, or I convince myself. Tonight, I seek out the cove. I seek out Becca. I feel so strongly I will find her there; nothing will tear me away from this path.

September 7th
Once again, I find myself facing the chatter of birds before dawn, but rather than woken, I've not yet slept. Journal, I must slow my hand, for I have such news to share! As promised, I set into the jungle following my last entry with naught but a vague sense of intuition. What was it Mother used to say? A woman's gut is her only source of truth. And I suppose once again she was right, for I needed no map, nor path, nor view of guiding stars. I walked for what must have been hours. Worldly light faded. The oppressive closeness of damp air turned from welcome respite from the day's heat to a lurid chill. Any fear I might have held, of being lost, of being attacked by some feral animal, of any other calamity that might befall a woman alone was chased away by insistent *knowing*. Onward I walked, and walked, and walked. Skin goosed, ankles chafed by unruly foliage. Glimmers of a shining moon were my only companion, and yet I felt less alone than I have in such time.

I then heard the distant roar of water on water and stone. Through a thicket of wide, tropical leaves, I spotted the cove and the waterfall feeding therein. In the dark, in the black, I sensed her there. This sensing, this *knowing* drew me to the water's edge. I gazed into the unknowable depths, first seeing only a reflection of myself by starlight, but then, journal, THEN a flash!

Ashen hair made translucent by clear water.

"Becca!" I called out to her, but she moved so quickly, more like a fish than a woman, I despaired that she might not possibly hear me, not over the roaring water. "Becca!" I called, again and again. "I've come, I'm here!" And, at last, in the place where the deluge poured into the cove, her head broke the surface. The waterline lapped beneath her nose, and those lilac eyes (I could have sworn they were lilac), seemed to glow like firebugs.

I removed my shoes. Mossy stone slick beneath my bare soles, I stepped forward, wishing deeply to join her in the water. But as the coolness licked my toes, Becca gave a curt shake of her head, and I understood that she wished me to come no closer. I was reminded then, of the skittish cat my uncle kept, and how it would run if I pursued, but would draw closer if I merely sat and practiced patience. So, I settled upon the stone, keeping perfectly still in hopes she would move toward me, that she would come close enough that I could explain, ask her forgiveness. Long moments passed. She watched, unmoving, draped in spray from the cascading falls. In my waiting, a spider with legs like spindles crept onto my calf. His thin arms grasped the meat of my leg, and I suppressed the impulse to swat him away. My persistence was fruitful. Becca lurched forward, as if pushing off some unseen rock, gliding toward me, black ripples fanning out behind her like she was some cunning eel.

When she was close enough to hear a soft murmur, I said, "I love you." Still, her mouth remained below water, but her gaze softened, and I detected some sadness there, some longing which mirrored my own. I again moved to join her in the water, but again she tipped her jaw, and I took it as disapproval. I stopped, but closer to the water as I was, I caught the image of her below.

Shredded flesh billowed with the water's movement around white bone. I glanced back to her face, bursting with life, then back to her body below, rotting. Becca nodded. I should've felt revulsion. My lover decomposed before me. I should've been overcome with grief, for surely only the dead may rot. But journal, I felt only longing: to cradle the flayed pieces of her, to run my fingers between her ribbons of flesh, to kiss her mouth whether I find succulent lips or grizzled sinew.

I prepared myself to dive. Whatever fate found Becca, let it find me too, I thought. Perhaps the void attempted to swallow her but got stuck in the chewing. No sooner did the thought prompt my body to move, than Becca beat me to the notion, diving herself into the unseen depths.

I waited, journal. Waited and waited. I called to her, then screamed myself hoarse. But Becca did not return to me. Not even the spider deigned to keep me company in my hysteria. So I made my way back to Mallory and Tim's, all the while considering the great void, the black leather book, my lover's decay. I pondered the diving bell spider, crafting an unlikely home beneath the surface, trapping a bubble of air within its web.

I must return to the book, to search its pages for some rite to return Becca to me in her truest form. I must listen closely at tonight's service. I must implore Mallory to talk to me, if I can.

I am too close, journal. I feel the breath of the void at my back. If love can snatch a woman from its jaw, then mine will salvage Becca.

September 7th (Evening)

Despite the flurry of emotion from my encounter with Becca (or perhaps because of it) sleep took me hard and fast in the early morning hours, a fact evidently frowned upon by Tim who woke me with a too loud, too close clearing of his throat.

"You'll be getting ready for service," he said, before trudging back to his room.

My manner of waking was abrupt, but I was glad for it, for without the intervention I may well have slept through my opportunity to ferret out more information about the goings on of Bell Harbor, and thus, lose my opportunity to snatch my lover from the jaws of her ill fate.

The church pews held the same faces, and the boy I questioned prior gave me a wide berth. I must confess I tuned out much of Sunday's sermon, focused intently on finding a local who I might press for information on Becca's whereabouts. But having confirmed this for myself, I listened attentively to the preacher's words (though, I know not whether he would have called himself preacher, for the message was unlike any I've heard in a Christian gathering).

Even with all my focus, I gleaned but bits and pieces of the message offered. He spoke of *appeasement* and made mention of the *great void,* between slipping into some foreign tongue. From the cadence, I knew it was not Latin, but it also lacked Germanic pronunciation and thus the origin escaped me. More remarkable than the words spoken, was what remained unspoken. No talk of *righteousness*, of *saviors*, of *sin.* And most disappointingly, no talk of *water women*. At the conclusion, the preacher lingered at his pulpit, the meager audience milling and sieving out with no great urgency. I approached the altar, feeling the eyes of Mallory and Tim upon me, but I dared not look back to discover whether it was impatience or chastisement in their glare. I balled my fists and summoned my strength, shifting my weight on the groaning floorboards to catch his attention.

"Father–" I started.

"Brother," he corrected.

"Brother, would you tell me of the women in the water?"

I braced for his dismissal, but it did not come. Instead, he raised a wiry, curious brow. "The water women do not call for you. You needn't concern yourself with them."

He turned to leave, but I caught him by the shoulder. "I concern myself with one."

He gave a knowing nod.

"Bring her back to me," was what tumbled out. For how could I explain? Desperate need pushed the words out without consideration for consequence.

"She chose freely the water," he said, and patted my head as if I was some discontented schoolboy, then retired to a back room. Knowing the conversation had ended, I did not pursue him. Rather, I joined Mallory and Tim at the foyer, anticipating questions.

None came.

Instead, Mallory recited what I recognized as a passage from the book she gifted me. This particular entry was penned in curving letters which together created a spherical pattern.

All friends begin as strangers,
Lovers as friends,
And lovers, most often, become strangers again.

I grew restless. Such vague and enigmatic responses drove me to ask forthright: "There is a woman in the water. Something has happened to her, some curse. Help me save her, please!" Fortunately, church goers had cleared the area, so only Mallory and Tim heard my plea.

"It's you needs saving," Tim said. "Not her."

My body went rigid. Perhaps they suspected my predilections and bristled against them. But Mallory's tone was kinder.

"It's a rare gift," she said, "to circle the pattern twice."

The walk to their home was silent after that. It was then I devised the makings of a plan. Some magic traps Becca within those waters. The idol in my hosts' kitchen must have some significance, some meaning. Perhaps it holds the power to break the spell. I arrived at Bell Harbor on my own, located the cove on my own. Why should I not also save Becca on my own?

While Mallory's words spun round in my head, my feet grew eager. I stopped only to pen this entry in case something goes awry. I will go straight away to the water. I will drag Becca from the depths if I must.

Fatigue dims my senses and sensibility. I know this. But I've wasted enough time, enough years of my life in a farce, denying my nature and my true joy. I'll not offer up another moment to a false god or societal expectation. I go to the jungle. To the cove. To Becca. And I go freely.

***

A letter from Mallory Daines to Sandra Harraway, dated September 8th

Mrs. Harraway,

Gemma Roberts is dead. I don't expect you'll believe the story of how she came to her end, but I'll relay it nonetheless. I hope you can put aside your grief and superstition enough not to seek rash action against Bell Harbor or our people.

As you well know, Gemma arrived with a singular ambition: to locate her friend, Rebecca. While she neglected to speak plainly, I gleaned she did, indeed, find Rebecca, in our most sacred cove. While your beliefs will impede you from digesting what I am to relay next, I invite you to put your religiosity aside. You may even find you gain greater knowledge of cosmic happenings by doing so.

Rebecca, or Becca as Gemma called her, had chosen to transcend. She became a vessel of the great void, which I don't expect you to understand. Caught between this life and the antithesis, she is equal parts woman and bone, creature and soul.

Gemma did not understand this. Not fully.

She wished to "save" Becca from this illustrious fate. So, when Gemma left our home and went into the jungle, I followed her. I hid behind the trunk of a gumbo limbo tree as Gemma approached the water's edge, calling out for her lover. I hope this is not a shock to your puritan sensibilities. We in Bell Harbor know it is quite natural for women to share love. Ripples in the water told me the women there heard her call, and that they grew more curious as Gemma removed her shoes.

A glowing set of eyes popped up from the depths, then another and another, until twenty sets peered at Gemma there on that stony outcropping. Gripping a mangrove limb to brace herself, Gemma leaned over the water, extending an arm toward its surface. She cried out, begging for Becca to take her hand. She proclaimed she would not, *could* not, "bear to face the world alone." Apologies fell like rain from her lips, for errors large and small. And Becca did hear her, for she came to the surface in the area just below where Gemma stood. It was then that Gemma began to sob, understanding, I think, that Becca either could not, or *would* not, leave the water.

Gemma drew a statue from the waist of her skirt. She'd stolen this token from my home–which I do not condone, but also understand her fragile, emotional state. She threw it into the pool. I can only guess she thought it held some magic that might release Becca and the other women residing there. It had no such result, of course. Even you, Mrs. Harraway, must realize no human can command forces such as these.

It was then that Becca reached back to her, extending a long, thin arm, and stopping just short of grasping Gemma's hand. Racked with sobs, Gemma leaned, the limb on which she held cracking under the strain.

I had no choice but to attempt to intervene. "Gemma come," I said in my most commanding tone. I wanted to spare her the fall. I had no wish to see her drown. You see, Mrs. Harraway, the women in the water have welcomed many men into the cove but are far less amenable to their leaving.

Gemma looked to me, a flush of panic staining her cheeks. "It's quite alright." I spoke then as if to a child, with a soft, whispering tone. It was enough to banish the fear from her wild eyes, but, I'm afraid, did not persuade her to move away from the water's edge.

Rather, she smiled.

She looked back to her lover, whose thin arm still grasped at the space between them. Gemma released the limb, reaching instead for her lover, who accepted her into her arms, who embraced her with ferocity while cool, clear water splashed up all around them. Though I couldn't see their mouths, I swear I felt each of the water women smile beneath the waterline as the lovers held one another. Gemma glanced back at me as if to wave farewell, and then the water women disappeared, taking Gemma with them.

You should know that I lingered there the better part of an hour, but nothing more than insects broke the surface.

This must all be a shock to you, which is why I enclosed the journal. I trust you'll read the entries and see this is not some fantastical story I've dreamed up to hide ulterior motives. I said in my opening that Gemma Roberts is dead, but only because I'm sure this will be your summation of events. I do send my condolences. But there is a saying in Bell, that all friends begin as strangers, lovers as friends, and that lovers, most often, become strangers again. Please know the great void encountered Gemma as a stranger, welcomed her as an old friend, and now holds her as a lover.

Should you ever wish to visit, I humbly offer to host you in my home.

Regretfully,
Mallory Daines

Part III:

Survive the Essex

Survive the Essex

Published in audio format by *Escape Your Fate Podcast*, February 2024

A mere two days into your voyage and the drumming of waves against the Essex's hull is an angry tune. Pollard, jacket pressed for his debut as captain, staggers about the deck, back forced into an unnatural, straight line as if to defy the effect of the rolling sea.

"Blessed, she is." He taps the weatherbeaten railing, which, of course, holds true. You cannot help but recall the discussion at port.

In need of repairs, you heard.

One last trip, then we'll see to it, you heard.

The Essex groans. Lightning splits the dark sky.

Pollard shouts, but you're in no need of his direction, nor your crewmates. Each man sets to securing the ship, turning like cogs in a well-oiled machine. Well-oiled. That's why you're out here, after all. To fetch the oil that turns the gears of this world. Chill seeps through the linen of your shirt, but you're no stranger to cold, having faced winters far harsher than this back home in Nantucket. You've sailed south as far as Cape Horn and have kissed the Arctic Circle in the north. Still, the wind blows something mighty, and on her breath a whisper. Shrugging it away, you tell yourself the warning you hear is, as you've told your crewmates, no more than the devilish influence of seafaring superstition.

Reed and Sheppard have already taken to the stairs when you hear Pollard's voice above the howling gusts, "Below deck!"

You scramble to follow, brushing against your fellow sailors as dampened daylight turns to near black. Beneath deck, the scent of sweaty bodies, the close feel of men afraid as the ship rises on a cresting wave, then falls. A floating feeling in your gut that lasts just long enough for you to cling to Petersen. His chin turns, eyes wide, but before he can rebuke you–the ship pitches left.

Left, left, left.

You're thrown, the weight of men landing on top of you, the benches you sat upon now glare at you from the port side wall. No, floor. Benches are on the floor.

The ship's been thrown.

"Knock down!" Pollard yells, as if you needed telling.

It's not your first. The sea is a great and terrible thing, tossing ships about like they were no more than nuisances. You know, logically, it's only a matter of time. The captain will guide you through, make sure Essex catches a wave at just the right angle to throw you back to rightness. And yet the terror knows no logic. It courses through your body like poison, speeding your pulse and shortening your breaths. Then the pain starts: a warm, radiating throb in your wrist that reaches toward your elbow. Reed. He landed on it.

Using your good arm, you thrust him off. He mutters something between a curse and an apology before rolling his weight off your hand. Once free, you clutch it close, and like a colony of one mind, your crewmates right themselves, one by one, best they can with Essex rolled on her ass. Rain beating against the hull would be soothing if not for the awkward angles.

"We been through worse before," Pollard says, "no doubt will again. Back to it, boys."

You swallow down the frustration, knowing you won't be catching whales in a knocked down ship, but back to it you go, moving smoothly as you can to the store room to collect supplies.

Once alone, you seize the opportunity to examine your arm. The swelling has started. Broken, likely. So you use your good arm to free a bandage from the medical kit, wrapping it–looser than you should–in a lame attempt to stabilize the injury.

A single arm can only carry so much hardtack. You swaddle it in a scrap of cloth and clutch it close to your chest like an infant. When you return to the lower main hold, Sheppard has lain blankets.

"We'll pass the night here if we must," Pollard says.

You select a wool throw as your bed, settling in a space beside a porthole window, tucking your store of hardtack in a crevice. It'll make a shit breakfast after a shit night of sleep. Beneath, the ocean churns. You think of that whisper on the wind, but push it away. To sail is one thing. So few jobs in Nantucket can provide, and this is one. But you'll not succumb to the superstitions of sea-faring men. You're a man of logic and principle. There is no fate beside the one you make for yourself, a summation of choices and the consequences which accompany each. The ocean is no enemy. It does not hold vendettas like spurned men.

It takes the better part of an hour to find a comfortable position. Between the curvature of the wall, fiddling with your bandage, the dissatisfied muttering of Reed and Sheppard, the demands of Pollard for quiet, and the insistent throbbing of your wrist, the night stretches long. But morning will come, of that much you're sure. And with it, Essex will shape its own fortune, free from the influence of pagan deities, Christian morays, old wive's tales.

***

An uneasy night gives way to a mockingly lovely day. Cloudless skies stretch on past the furthest reaches of the horizon, a too-gleeful sun bearing down as Essex lies limply on her port side. Nickerson, a greenhorn, tries feebly to lift the mood.

"It's only a job, mates. Let's rest up while we can."

"You fucking fool," Reed says. "You think we might turn up with naught but a suntan and return home with full pockets?"

Nickerson stares blankly. Reed is cruel but you've not the energy to offer a gentler explanation.

"We're paid based on the catch. We catch nothing? We get nothing. Understand?"

Nickerson sucks his cheek between his jaws and chews.

"Fucking greenhorns." Reed attempts a dramatic exit, but stumbles over a length of rope on his way, significantly dampening the effect of the storm off.

Drawn to the commotion, Pollard spits out instructions: what type of wave to look for, the angle you need to catch it, etc. It's a tense morning. Hours of watching made longer by the incessant throb in your arm, the wrapping and rewrapping which does little to dull it. But as daylight reaches its height, you find your mark. A generous wave tosses Essex back onto her keel, and this small victory is enough to brighten spirits aboard.

"Take stock," Pollard says.

Sheppard and Reed head below deck, but you remain above, volunteering to count the whaling boats. As you suspected, four have been lost. Thankfully most of the food stores remain, the pigs aboard are no worse for wear, and when a spark of hope is lit within you, it's fanned to full flame when first mate Chase shouts, "Whale!"

A flurry of footsteps to the starboard side. He's a magnificent beast, perhaps the largest you've seen.

"Gushing with spermaceti, that one is!" Chase says, near drooling.

Out of instinct, Chase and Joy move for the harpoon, but your gaze breaks from them when a massive strike shakes the Essex.

"We've been stove!" Pollard cries.

The sound of wood splintering throughout her hull is a surreal thing, something your years at sea have not prepared you for. The whale, three times longer than the ship and twice in girth, is a monstrous shadow beneath the waterline. You brace. Will Essex crack? Snap in half like a splinter of driftwood?

The whale dives, its massive shadow dimming as it disappears into the deep. Utter silence as the crew holds its breath.

Then a collective exhale. The splintering stops. Essex calms. A wash of relief gives way to the present moment, and Chase, Joy, and Nickerson join you on the starboard side. Together you peer into the blackness below.

"A monster, that one," says Joy.

"A damned prize," says Chase..

"A devil." Did it come from Nickerson? Or was it another whisper on the wind?

No. No wind today.

"We should be checking the damage," Pollard says, the strain of disappointment clear in his tone. This whale alone would've made up for the knock down, its spermaceti now wasted, fated to rot in the things carcass when it meets its watery end.

Chase and Joy turn to inspect the lower decks for damage.

"You ever seen a whale hit a ship?"

"Nay."

"And me neither," Chase says.

Nor have you heard of such a thing: a whale attacking a ship? But you shrug it off. A fluke, you think. Nothing more. You step away from the railing, prepared to take your post as mast to control position, when there's movement in your periphery. A great, looming shape darkens the sea.

It's back.

You snatch up a lance, pull your injured limb to your side and call out, "Whale!"

The beast is close. Close enough to hit, but also close to the rudders. Too close. If you strike it now, the fin out could render the ship inoperable. But it's so, so close. And Reed was right: your payday's only as rich as your hull is full.

You've a choice to make: Lance the whale, or Let it go?

To Lance the Whale, advance to page 153.

To Let it Go, advance to page 167.

Lance The Whale

It's as natural as anything for a man of your experience to thrust the spear into the whale's head. Even with your injury it's an easy target, close enough to jump upon its back should you leap from where you stand, and large enough that even a man with terrible aim would hit his mark. As if on cue, three lances follow, launched by Chase, Reed, and Sheppard in turn. Pollard looks on from the foremast.

The beast begins to fin out, flailing a tail that dwarfs any you've seen into the keel.

"Chimney's afire!" Chase calls, a hint of snark in his tone.

And indeed, blood erupts from the whale's spout, a demonic volcano of gore that stains the ocean.

"Saved us a Nantucket sleigh ride today, eh?" Chase slaps you on the back. "Fucker's so stupid, didn't even need the harpoon."

But a haze settles over what should be your joyous celebration. It was too close. And in the beast's desperate fight to stave off its demise, a distinct crack.

"That'll be the rudder," you say.

Chase swats away your concern, but the color leeches from Reed, and Sheppard swallows hard.

"Captain," Reed says.

Pollard joins you starboard side, unable to take his eyes off the whale's dance with death, groans splitting the eerily calm afternoon in two.

"The rudder," you repeat.

Pollard spits over the rail toward the beast, but if it lands its mark, it's impossible to tell, the sea dark with blood and foaming with froth from the frantic movements.

"Nickerson," he says, "you and Sheppard ready the whaling boat, take the blubber hooks. You're on flensing. Reed, Chase, Prepare the tryworks. Coffin," he gives you a steely eye, "come with me. We'll see just how bad the bitch stove us."

"Aye."

"Aye."

The men set about their tasks as you follow your captain. Somewhere deep you know the rudder is lost. You wind your way to the taffrail, and when Pollard confirms as much, you know you're not much better off than a bloated corpse at the mercy of the tides. The Essex may not be sunk, but with no ability to steer her, you're at the mercy of fickle winds.

"We'll wait to tell them," Pollard says. "Let them enjoy the catch. Leave it to me."

You'd no intention of breaking the news to the crew, but all the same, dread creeps up the back of your neck like a chill despite the hot day.

Piece by piece, the thing is drawn aboard. Trying out fills the air with a thick stench. The process of boiling the blubber to turn it to oil is a ghastly one, but the crew smells only money. The deck is slick with blood, speckled with bits of carcass. Sheppard and Reed seem to revel in it, caressing hunks of yellow fat in their meaty hands as they transport it for processing. But for all the gore and strangeness around blubber, it pales in comparison to the retrieval of the largest prize.

It takes six men in total to haul the beast's head aboard. Ropes and chains and a system of pulleys make it possible; all the ingenuity of man is needed to flay nature's largest animal. But when the head is thumped on deck, you see not ingenuity, but something closer to lust. Pollard, Reed, Sheppard, Joy, and Chase alike glare at the disembodied thing like a long lost lover.

"Chase," Pollard says, anointing his first mate the honor.

Chase is all too eager to step forward, whacking the skull and cracking it open. Inside, white gold. No, more precious than gold. A liquid so valuable it lured you from house and home for the year long journey. Spermaceti.

Chase sets to work bailing out the waxy substance with a bucket, the others following suit. "Must be near 500 gallons in there."

Pollard's eyes flutter. It seems to you, this is nearly an erotic experience for him.

Candles, ointments, cosmetics. You can scarcely imagine how this substance, smelling of fresh milk and requiring so much violence to retrieve, could be used for such purposes. And yet, it must be. For why else would it fetch such a high price?

The sight of such great quantity is a respite from the cold truth of your situation. But you can't escape for long. It creeps back in, slow and steady as a rising tide: You are stuck. You may be rich in whale fat, but you'll die rich in whale fat if you don't do something.

Even rich men can't survive forever adrift at sea. The ocean will swallow you–pockets full or penniless–just the same.

***

Pollard breaks the news after the men have eaten supper. Reed's fork hovers in mid air, a bit of pork dropping back down to his plate. Sheppard huffs and shrugs his shoulders, but the feigned apathy doesn't mask a wild look in his eye. Nickerson doesn't seem to understand, looking to the veteran crewmates to gauge the seriousness. Joy and Chase talk in whispers.

"We'll take to the whale boats," Pollard says. "If we stack supplies we should make it to Easter Island." He offers the opportunity for dissent, but none do, understanding that floating on a rudderless ship is tantamount to a death sentence. The sailors are divided into groups of six, and you and the men gather hardtack, whale meat, navigation equipment, and fresh water before abandoning Essex, pigs, blubber, and all.

Sheppard and Reed talk in low voices, eying Chase intermittently to see if the first mate can hear.

"We spent all day trying out. Lugging that blubber on deck. Why'd Pollard let us go to all the trouble?" Sheppard says.

"He's a wiry fuck," Reed answers.

"The fat's rendered. We'll get to Easter Island, come back with supplies, repair Essex. Don't let a bit of bad luck go to your heads," you say. Tensions are high enough, you don't need the crew turning on one another.

"Bad luck? Ill omens, I'd say." Sheppard looks onto the horizon as if watching a ghost.

"Let's not–"

"You shut your mouth," Reed says. "No better than a greenhorn, you are."

Instead of biting back, you fold your arms across your chest. "It was just a storm," you mutter. But once again the hairs at your nape are raised. You have felt it too, the heavy presence of looming misfortune.

Steering the boats away from Essex is a matter of navigating through quickly turning hunks of meat and floating islands of viscera. The crew brought aboard the most lucrative pieces of the beastly whale, but hundreds of pounds of the thing still float around you. A single fin breaks the surface. Sharks. Of course, sharks. You've left a feast for them. Inching closer to the center of the boat, you try not to think of the tales you've heard: sharks overturning boats and snapping up the sailors inside. *They'll be sated with the whale meat,* you tell yourself. But another voice, a low hum on the wind says otherwise. *Sharks are never sated. They're like men in that way, always hungry, always hunting their next meal.*

***

Days pass. Reed and Sheppard repeat the same stories you've heard one hundred times. Chase keeps quiet mostly. The other whale boats drift in and out of sight. Early on, the men would call out to one another, but as the water ran short and the nights grew long and cold, the talk amongst boats dropped off.

The sea has been unkind. Tall waves break over the sides, soaking the hardtack in saltwater. You warn the other men against eating it, especially with water so low, but they eat it anyway, flashing their savage smiles at you while they chew. Your sunburnt flesh is tight and itchy. Reed's nose has all but peeled off in the middle. Sheppard's eyes drawn into a permanent squint. Your tongue hardens in your mouth: the rations are necessary but strict. It starts to swell. Sharks circle in the hundreds, their fins cutting through the surface like knives through thin glass. Hope has almost faded entirely when Joy, from another boat calls, "Land ho!"

"Easter Island?" you ask.

Chase squints against reflected sunlight bouncing off the waves. "Could be."

"About damn time," Reed growls.

Sheppard elbows him in the ribs. "Lack of beauty sleep is really starting to take its toll, eh?"

"Fuck you." The curse is a rasp. Reed has barely the energy for a threat.

Approaching the island is slow and torturous, but as you reach shore, this much is clear: this is not Easter Island. Nevertheless, the feeling of sand beneath your feet is very welcome. Whale boats arrive on shore one by one, the men jumping out with renewed fervor for life. Some hug the sand. Some spit into the lapping waves. Some shake fists at sea deities. All breathe a sigh of relief.

Nesting birds litter the shorelines, and the men are greedy for them, them and the eggs they guard. Salty hardtack and barely cooked whale meat will keep them alive, but it's far from a balanced diet. As Nickerson builds a fire, Joy and Sheppard take to hunting birds like school boys, running and squawking at them, capturing them in deadly bear hugs, raiding the nests. They've gathered enough to feed all twenty men when they return.

For your part, you find a small spring. If you dig, it's enough to bail out water to wash down the bird meat, and the men grant you a hero's welcome when you return with a bucket of water. They needn't know it took you twice as long as it would've anyone else, scooping and flailing with your one good hand. As day gives way to dusk, celebration turns to planning.

"If it ain't Easter Island, where the hell are we?" Reed asks.

Pollard straightens his posture, unwilling to look a fool. "The winds must have taken us slightly off course. I'm sure Easter Island is within sailing distance."

"You want us back in those boats? We nearly died out there," Nickerson says, worry traced on the lines in his forehead.

"You s'pose we should just move in here?" Sheppard asks with a sneer.

"No." Nickerson sits back on his heels.

"We'll rest up, restock, get our strength back," Pollard says. "Then we'll vote on what to do from there."

The men nod in agreement, stuffing their mouths with stringy bird meat, oil slicking their chins. Reed pops an egg in his mouth whole. You can't help but hope he chokes on it.

***

Two weeks pass. Where once the beach was littered with nests, there are now only a few with occupants. A fortnight's time and the bird population is decimated. When Joy returns from a hunt with barely enough meat for half of you, the conversation turns again to planning.

"We won't last here much longer," Chase says.

It's what you've all been thinking, waiting until the last possible moment to say it aloud. And that moment is now.

"We'll need to head to Easter Island," Pollard says, a foregone conclusion. But even as he says it, his gaze falls to Peterson, who's taken to lying most days in the shade, his health turning ill from the stress and the strain of the days at sea.

"We can't all go," Nickerson says, avoiding looking at Peterson directly.

"Aye," Pollard agrees. "We'll take a vote. A few will remain here. Should be enough food and water to sustain a small group until we can return to pick you up. The rest of us take what supplies we can and get back in the whale boats.

You look around, from your haggard ship mates to the sparse shoreline. *Not fate*, you tell yourself. *Just choices and the consequences that come with them.*

"Who'll be staying?" Pollard asks.

You wonder whether the sharks still fill the waters, whether you could survive here long enough for rescue, whether Pollard can make it to Easter Island and send rescue at all. *Choices,* you think. *And their consequences.*

You have a choice to make now: Stay on the island? Or get back in your whale boat?

To get back in your whale boat, advance to page 161.
To stay on the island, advance to page 165.

Get in the Whale Boat

Nickerson stays with Peterson, Wright, and Chapple. A shame, as despite being a greenhorn, he's the only man with a temperament that matches yours. Once again you're paired with Chase, Reed, and Sheppard. While Chase's health seems somewhat restored from his time on the island, Reed and Sheppard have yet to lose their feral looks. If anything, they have been made more bloodthirsty by their time hunting birds.

While you said nothing to the others, the image of Reed, catching a gull in his arms and tearing into its bare neck while it squealed and struggled is one you won't soon forget, and you can't help but wonder whether he'd show you the same brutality if given the chance.

A curtain of clouds obscure the sun's glare. You've an impulse to call it a gift from some benevolent deity, but push this away, just another shade of that same superstition you've seen rear its illogical head in your fellow sailors. Even in the faded light, shark fins are visible in the chop, appearing regularly as flotsam. Whether they've been riled by the now distant whale carcass, or these waters are their territory, the threat is palpable.

Reed makes a mockery of it. Dipping his hand over the boat's side, feigning a bite, only to whirl it back out unharmed, splashing you with seawater each time. The joke seems to never grow old for him and Sheppard, but each time the water licks your face, leaving traces of salt across your upper lip and stinging your already dry eyes, resentment builds. If Chase notices, he says naught. Joy and Pollard's boats have drifted out of sight, leaving him to navigate using equipment alone.

"Hope the Captain's kept eyes on Joy and his crew," he says.

"Hope not," Reed says.

Chase shoots him a cold look.

"When we get back to Essex, less men to split the profits with, eh?"

Chase gives a disapproving shake of his head as Sheppard chuckles.

"And what do you say, Coffin?" Reed and Sheppard look to you. "Joy and his men ought to have not busted up their equipment, aye? But we'll be no worse for wear should they drift out to sea." He wriggles his fingers up and away.

You inhale deep and hold your tongue.

"He's got nothin' to say, do he?" Sheppard says. "After all, it's his fault we're in this mess to begin with."

Reed raises an accusing brow. They exchange furtive looks, as if this isn't the first time they've raised this discussion. An anxious thread snakes its way through your core. You knew this might happen. Desperate men need someone to blame. You're spared having to respond when something bumps the boat. Not enough to tip it, but enough to throw all off balance. Righting yourself, you say what the men already know.

"Sharks."

Sheppard licks his lips. "They make a fine soup, you know."

"Can we talk about naught but food?" Chase's patience with them grows thin, but perhaps he too suspects the violent capabilities of the pair, and averts his gaze as if indicating he's not looking for a fight.

Reed reaches into his jacket pocket, withdrawing a hunk of hardtack. "Pretty tired of this salty shit."

"Aye," Sheppard says.

"A soup would make for nice variety."

"Aye."

You intercede. "And how do you suppose we catch them, Reed?" You cast glances around for emphasis. "Do you see any harpoons?"

It's enough to quiet them for the moment, Reed lowering the brim of his cap and leaning back to catch an afternoon nap and Sheppard contenting himself with fidgeting with an errant strand on his trousers.

"How far, would you say?" you ask Chase in a low tone.

"A week," he mutters. "Perhaps two."

***

Four weeks come and go, taking with them any shred of human decency that might have once dwelled in Reed and Sheppard. Chase said nothing when Sheppard held you down and raided your pockets for bits of hardtack and spoilt bird meat. The only water you've drunk is what you could catch in your palms during afternoon showers.

For the past several days, Reed and Sheppard have taken to fashioning fishing line out of strips of their tattered clothing. You thought, at first, it was an exercise in boredom, but when Sheppard draws a hook from his bag, you have to ask.

"You plan to fish with any empty hook? Seen naught but sharks, doubt the tuna will bite without a lure."

A sinister smirk curls Reed's lip. "Since all that talk of shark fin soup, my craving's grown."

"You'd have a hard time hooking even a curious shark with a bare hook," you say.

Sheppard chimes in, "And who says it'll be bare?"

Reed draws a knife from his jacket. "I heard stories, sure you all have, 'bout men stuck adrift, eating one another to stay alive." He draws the blade across his palm.

The thread of anxiety that started weeks back has grown to a rough cord, wrapping itself around your chest and innards.

It's enough to spur Chase to speak. "You don't plan to—"

"Eat Coffin here?" He flicks the blade's tip toward you. "And how might that satisfy my shark fin craving? "

You swallow hard. "It wouldn't."

"Indeed," Sheppard says.

"No," Reed continues. "I've somethin' else in mind."

In a practiced motion, Sheppard launches himself on top of you, holding your arms and pressing his weight onto your chest. You flail, but weakened by the limited food and water, you're no stronger than a flopping fish beneath his hold. Then a sharp stripe of pain at your ankle. Sawing pressure and hot liquid, and the high pitched scream that's all around. It's coming from you, you realize. Kick and fight as you must, it's no use. Reed, blocked by Sheppard's body, works his knife through your flesh, your nerves, your bone. When you realize he's taking your right foot, the world goes black.

***

You wake to brilliant blue sky. A tourniquet's been tied around your calf, and the bottom of the whale boat is layered in your jellified blood. As your vision comes into focus, you watch Sheppard stringing white meat onto his hook. Foggily, you wonder where it came from, bright red with fresh blood.

"Makes little sense to kill ya," Reed says.

Chase is pale despite the layers of scaly tan.

"When we can keep ya alive, you know, to draw in the real prize."

Sharks have gathered in even greater numbers, circling the whaling boat and eying Reed's makeshift fishing line.

"It's shark fin soup tonight, boys." Reed slaps Sheppard's back, and they join together in a chorus of twisted laughter before going abruptly silent.

"Fish on!" Reed calls.

Stay on the Island

After watching Reed catch a gull with his bare hands and tear out its throat with his gnashing teeth, it's not a difficult decision for you to stay on the island. He was a cruel man to start, and the prospect of sharing a confined space with him and his acolyte, Sheppard, is less than enticing. You, Nickerson, and Peterson watch the whale boats depart, one by one, after a slight scuffle around Joy losing his navigation equipment.

When the boats have turned to specks on the horizon, Nickerson says a prayer for their safe return. Despite your agnostic leaning, you bow your head and fold your hands. Peterson lies upon a burlap sack in the shade. He won't be much good for hunting, nor conversation. Fading in and out of consciousness, you don't know how long he'll survive the elements, but resolve yourself to providing for him as best you can.

Nickerson and you take turns collecting water and searching for nests. Those along the beach are destroyed, but you venture into the treeline and manage to find a few eggs. When you return to the campsite, Nickerson is preparing to boil water over a weak flame.

"That all?" he asks, a downtrodden look at the three measly eggs.

You nod.

"We'll have to figure something out."

Eggs and water boiled, you have a slight lunch, one egg for each of you, then get to work on whittling down a few strong sticks to create spears. It takes a few knicks and the better part of the day, but just before sundown you've each got a workable weapon. Trodding into the shallows, the silver schools of fish move like lightning, and after a few useless throws, you wonder whether creating the spears was a fool's errand. But just as the last licks of light begin to fade, Nickerson cries out.

"Fish! Dammit, I got a fish!"

It's a tiny thing, barely enough meat to suck from the fragile bones, but it's something. It's hope. Unable to rouse Peterson from his sleep, you share the meat between the two of you.

"Helluva first trip," you say.

Nickerson laughs. It's a sound you thought you might never hear again, a sweet thing that bounces across the air between you.

If some benevolent deity does exist, it smiles on you. Over the next week, you find a tidepool rich with crabs and mussels. Their tender flesh has the sweetest taste! And Nickerson, something of an amateur engineer, crafts a well when the water runs short, rigging a pulley system to ease water retrieval. It's far from an island getaway, but you've all you need to sustain yourselves. The same, unfortunately, cannot be said for Peterson. He has n't woken in days. So, when flies collect around his mouth and eyes one morning, you're saddened but not surprised to find he'd passed in the night.

Nickerson makes fine company. He's a sharp witted man and fills the long evening hours with stories both real and imagined. You impart to him your knowledge from years at sea, secrets usually hidden from greenhorns. And when, on the fourth week, a cloud on the horizon takes an unusual shape, you stare at it together. When it seems to square off at each end, you each say nothing, but watch as it draws closer. When a red and white flag and a strong wooden hull come into focus, tears fill your eyes, but still it feels too fragile, too tenuous to say it.

So you don't.

But on the tip of each of your tongues are the words, *we are saved*.

Let it Go

You let the whale pass unharmed. A breath of relief passes the lips of Chase and Joy in unison, and as the massive, dark shape disappears, you drop your lance.

Pollard sucks his teeth, perhaps thinking of the blubber now lost to the waves, but as he opens his jaw to chide you, his eyes dart left. You spin to follow Pollard's gaze, and find the bull whale has turned and now speeds toward the port bow. Watching in disbelief, you and the crew say nothing, unable to stop the creature from ramming the hull.

You think to grab the lance once more, but as you bend to grab it, you're thrown onto your head and shoulder, the Essex shaking from the force of the beast's strike.

"Stove!"

"Stove!"

Woozy from the fall, you hear the cry from numerous voices, unable to pinpoint who's speaking. A groan from the keel. The first strike caused splintering, but from the deep bellows of Essex, this hit is something else entirely.

"To the whale boats," Pollard cries. "We're sunk."

You scramble to your feet, trying desperately to make sense of it. A whale? Attacking a ship? It's unheard of, and yet, the men scurry to the remaining whale boats, and you follow suit. Keeping your footing is as difficult as it might be in any great squall. The bow's dipped below the waves, the deck now pitched at an extreme angle. Water rushes past the railing, soaking your boots. When you get to the whale boat, Sheppard, Chase, Reed, and Nickerson are already inside. And they push off away from the failing Essex before your boot has fully left the deck.

Having a remarkably pragmatic head upon his shoulders, Nickerson had the good sense to grab a stash of hardtack before climbing aboard. He doles it out in rations, and though it's soaked in seawater, each man clutches the food greedily. Ten minutes, and the Essex is sunk. You can scarcely believe the speed at which she disappeared beneath the sea, and at the hands of what you thought was your prey. Swimming through the chop are two pigs who escaped their pens. You help Chase to wrestle them on board, another food source, if it comes to it.

The crew brings the three whale boats together and takes stock of inventory. Enough food for a few weeks, but not nearly enough fresh water. Two boats have navigation equipment, Joy's does not. Pollard commands Joy stay within sight of the other boats, lest he be lost to the current, and Joy agrees with a somber nod.

Maps are drawn out, and Pollard along with his first and second mate study the possible courses. As they discuss, you notice Reed and Sheppard are eying you with distaste. When you meet Reed's gaze, he spits overboard, a pointed slight.

"Should've lanced the beast," he says.

"It was well within range," Sheppard adds.

"The rudder–" you start but are interrupted when Pollard clears his throat.

"The Marquesas are the closest island chain," Pollard says. The group falls silent, then exchanges whispers. You need not hear the details to know what they say. It's a prominent superstition amongst whaling men, that the Marquesas are host to an array of horrors. Men who bed one another, who eat each other's flesh. Tall tales and puritanical nonsense, you think, and have never seen any evidence to prove contrary. But belief in ill omens, influence of deities, and fear of cannibalism and *unnatural* predilections comes as easily to seafaring men as hyperbolic recounts of their catch.

Pollard then continues. "A bit further off, but still within reach, is Easter Island. A safe port, as we know." A few heads nod amongst the whale boats. "I leave it to a vote. We risk the Marquesas and the islanders therein, or we risk the sea and make the longer trip to Easter Island."

A slew of hands shoot up in favor of the shorter trip. Another slew for Easter Island. It falls to you to break the tie.

Do you head to the Marquesas or make the longer trip to Easter Island?

To head to Marquesas, advance to page 171.
To make the trip to Easter Island, advance to page 175.

Head to the Marquesas

You vote for the Marquesas, knowing confidently that the myth and superstition of the people who reside there are just that, and to risk extra time on open sea could easily result in a death sentence. What you don't mention is how your lameness makes the prospect of rowing even to the relatively close island chain a Herculean task.

"It is decided," Pollard says. "Set course for the Marquesas."

Having voted for Easter Island, Reed and Sheppard's ire for you is only inflamed. Nickerson offers a sympathetic look as they stare daggers. You pretend to be distracted by the chop, but of course you feel their eyes. Joy holds his oar aloft, knowing he must stay within sight of Pollard or Chase's boats, and waiting to see whether the captain or first mate will lead the slog. It's Pollard, in the end. With a firm nod, the men in his boat strike the chop, propelling their whaleboat forward into the seemingly endless blue.

You clench your jaw to hide the wince as you paddle. Reed settles where he can glance easily in your direction with each stroke. Who might've won in a melee on an ordinary day would be anyone's guess, but with your arm still purpled and twice its usual size, any betting man would know better than to risk coin on you. So, you swallow what you want to say. Minutes then hours pass in patterns of oar strokes, in intermittent drops of sweat into your lashes.

"'Course this one'd choose the Marquesas," Reed says.

Chase pretends not to hear, running his fingertips through a bit of sea foam.

"More of his ilk," Shepard says.

Splinters dig into your palm, knuckles turning white from the force of your grip.

"Save your energy," Chase says.

It's enough to quiet the pair of them, and while they're not looking, you roll your eyes at the irony. If there ever were two men in love, surely it was Shepard and Reed. The pace slows as night falls, and Joy tosses a rope to your boat to keep from drifting while the men catch a few precious hours of rest. You're sure you'll lie awake, the acrid scent of urine wafting up from the hull, but to your surprise, sleep takes you quickly and deeply, and when you wake it's to hoarse voices calling one another.

The rope is gone.

Joy is gone.

There's a back and forth, questions of whether to remain in place and hope Joy and his men might find a way to navigate back. But the argument unspoken eventually wins out: Without navigation equipment, without line of sight, they're as good as dead; and you will be too, unless you row.

The tips of your fingers on the injured arm have turned an unnatural shade of indigo by the first week. The almondy smell of rot permeates your tongue by the second. Reed opens his mouth to taunt you, only to gag on the airborne taste of your rotting flesh.

The others say nothing when you stop rowing.

You take to long hours staring over the starboard side, into the black depths. You let the sun's reflection burn your irises. Once, you think you spot a school of silvery fins below. You think of joining them. Extending both palms toward the water's welcoming, open mouth, it would be so easy to slip inside. Perhaps the fish would be friendly, you think, the saltwater good for your arm.

"Land ho!"

The voice comes from afar. Pollard's boat, you realize. You snatch yourself back from the edge of oblivion.

"Land ho!" he calls again.

You squint against the horizon.

"We'll make shit meals for the locals," Reed grumbles. His papery skin stretches tight over protruding bone. He lacks the energy for real wit, even for real fear. He keeps rowing.

The boat slides from black ocean to deep navy to teal. Trees sway on an island breeze. The tiny specks of human bodies come into focus on the shore. Whether you row toward death doesn't matter when you're certainly rowing away from it.

When Chase jumps from the ship, he's in waist deep water. It's only then it sinks in: You're out of open water. You've made it to land. Reed and Shepard follow, trudging in an awkward line behind Pollard and the men in his boat. Rolling your way off the whaleboat, you meet the shallow water with a splash, and despite all your assurances to the contrary, you wonder if next you'll feel the tips of arrows penetrate your back.

But you buoy up. Wipe the saltwater from your eyes. Pollard's firmly on shore, the other men close behind him. Islanders rush to meet them, offering towels, offering water, offering steadying hands. The tide laps around your ankles. Your palm is black, shot through with angry red lines. A canteen is thrust to your peeling lips.

You are saved.

Head to the Easter Island

You'll not be further victim of Reed's taunting and suspicions. To cast a vote in favor of the Marquesas would only confirm, in his mind and Sheppard's, your indecent love of other men. Even the draw of safety is not enough to stave off their threat, narrow eyes cutting accusing daggers as you consider the choice before you. But it has already been made–by puritanical value and tradition, by superstition and the wild tales of sea-faring men.

"To Easter Island," you say.

Reed's shoulders fall as if releasing the jab he had at the ready. You exhale a smooth and steady breath of relief, but it's not fully escaped your lips when the oars dipping into the sea to turn you stir what should have been, all along, the more present fear: Easter Island is twice the distance. You've only two pigs and saltwater logged hardtack amongst a slew of frustrated men. The shadow of the whale, gone from the sea but not from your mind, fills the air with abandoned promise. The invisible specter of would-be riches, the ghost of a paycheck, is enough to make you grab the oars, your injured arm be damned, and start rowing.

Without navigation equipment, Joy's boat struggles to keep itself within sight of you. Should yours and Pollard's boats drift out of eyeline, Joy will be at the mercy of the wind. But somehow you've no empathy in you to slow. The wind whispers, *You could've lanced it, filled the hull with blubber and spermaceti.* Fear, that the others hear that same taunting, pushes you forward, reaches like fingers at the back of your neck. Sharp pain shoots from wrist to elbow. You clench your jaw to ignore it, and think you hear your molars cracking. A breeze tells you it will be just enough. *Just enough*, it says, *to push Reed to do what he's always wanted to. To rile Sheppard into his fold. Just enough, to frighten Chase into inaction.* So you row.

Faintly, you hear Joy calling out, but you don't turn back. You row. Even when the pain turns to fire in your forearm, you row. Even when a warm trickle circles your wrist like a bracelet, you row. Until your movements fall wild and uneven, your oar strokes more hindrance than help, and Chase grips your shoulders.

"Time for a break," he says, tugging the oars away from your white knuckle hold.

Your focus becomes your own once more as the first mate takes over, doing his best to ignore the crimson stain in the wood. Glancing back, you find nothing. Hear nothing but the wind slipping past your ears.

"Joy?" you ask.

Chase clears his throat, dipping the oars in and out twice before responding, "He'll be along."

Sheppard surrenders his oars to Reed, the two of them exchanging a knowing look. You strain your ears against the wind and dipping of oars and lapping of waves and heavy silence. No voice. Nothing from Joy's boat. Only then do you check your injury, unwrapping the bandage to take stock of the damage. What was swollen and bruised is now a shining, angry thing, shot through with red and streaks of purple. Your eyes follow the streak of blood, already drying, to where a sliver of bone pokes through muscle and flesh. The size and shape of an incisor, you think, as if your own arm is smiling at you, winking at you.

Sheppard must notice it too, for he tears a strip of cloth from his own shirt tail and tosses it to you. "You should cover that back up. Don't need you turning black and rotted out here too."

So the whale is on his mind, and yet, a shred of kindness. You tie the strip of fabric around the worst of your injury, covering the wound's toothy smile. Perhaps infection sets in, or perhaps fatigue of the day catches up to you, but time slips like oil in water, and whether you slept or simply fell into black, when you wake it's morning, sun rearing a vengeful head over choppy seas. Your lips move to say, *Joy?* But all that comes forth is a rasp. Still, Chase seems to take your meaning, lowering his chin and giving you a somber shake. He's gone, then. He and his men.

You wait for the sorrow to step forward. It never does. Perhaps swallowed by the vacuous ache. A distant squeal leads you to think Pollard's boat must be slaughtering one of the pigs, and your fingers dig mindlessly into your gut which bellows in response to the sound. A pig's scream and a grumble. Call and answer.

Worship on the seas. Does the thought come from your own mind? Or is it another of the wind's malicious whispers?

Reed and Sheppard are deep in hypotheticals about what their next meal might be, were they at shore. And Chase steers the whaleboat toward Pollard's, where handfuls of still bloody pork are passed between men. You receive them, hand over hand, the soft musculature squishy and digging beneath your nails. Another grumble before your stomach turns. You consider the feel of the mush between your teeth, sliding over your tongue, the coppery taste slipping down your gullet and oozing into your belly. Reed and Sheppard don't seem to think much of it as they bite down into gelatinous fistfuls, gore staining their chins.

Chase teases out a strip of muscle from the surrounding tendon, holding it in the air like a worm before carefully placing it between his molars and swallowing quickly. A glance at your arm reveals more purple tendrils snaking through the shiny, red flesh. The metallic scent of raw meat mingles with the almondy aroma wafting up from your arm. You should look beneath the strip of fabric. You should, but you cannot.

Weeks pass.

The blubbery pig meat runs out.

The hardtack leaves a salty film on your lips and dwindles to nothing.

A greenhorn dies on Pollard's boat.

They say they buried him at sea. In the dark of the night. But the hollows beneath their eyes seem less sunken, their flesh less yellowed.

Why at night? When no one else could see?

You no longer question whether it's your own mind, the wind, or superstition breathed into life by dire circumstance. You let the questions come.

Sheppard and Reed try and fail to fish. The last of the pig innards have baked in the sun, drifting off their hooks with the slightest movement of a wave.

"We need bait," Reed grumbles, drawing another empty hook back to the whaleboat.

Purple fades to black at your fingertips. Puss oozes from your arm and collects in a puddle beneath you. Chase no longer asks you to row, so you slip in and out of sleep, no regard for the placement of sun or moon. Time bleeds into merciless haze, and bones protrude from the men's shirt collars.

Sheppard fiddles with an empty hook, refracting sunlight in and out of your eyes. Reed digs a pocket knife under a hangnail, wincing ever so slightly when a bead of blood forms on his thumb. You're faintly aware of your boat joining with Pollard's, of the stern faces and grim looks exchanged by your crewmates. When strips of paper are collected in a jar, you pay little attention to the conversation, too fascinated by the midnight colors your arm has turned. When the jar is shoved under your nose, you pluck a strip out, as you've noticed others doing in your periphery. Black spots snake their way to your shoulder. The scent of almond. The scent of brine. The scent of rot.

A black spot marks your strip of paper.

A flurry of eyes fix upon you: an uncanny mixture of pity and ravenous need. Reed folds his fingers around the handle of his knife. His eyes fall to a delicate spot on your neck.

"Whale," he says.

Epigraph

To the men reading this,

It wasn't personal.

Well—

Content Warnings

John List Would Like to Cancel His Subscription to Omaha Steaks
    Allusion to child death

Rusalnaya
    Murder, sexual content, body horror

I Am Not The Ghost You Wanted
    Sexual context

Giltiné
    Death, sexual content, gore

Between Her Teeth
    Sexual content, vore, cannibalism, reference to off-page sexual assault

A Fine Wife, Indeed
    Murder, Rumination about sexual assault

I Gave My Heart to a Hurricane
    Sexual content, gore

Eyes Open, Knees Apart for the End of the World
    Sexual content, gore

A Curse in the Midnight Zone
   Sexual content, internalized homophobia, gore

Backseat Driver
   Gore, implied murder of a domestic partner

Write My Eulogy On The Gloryhole Bathroom Stall
   Blasphemy, graphic sexual content, mutilation, addiction metaphor

Mulberry Silk
   Murder

Common Oleander
   Murder, gore

Of Ash and Soot
   Child endangerment

Gemma Prepared to Dive
   Internalized homophobia, implied suicide

Survive the Essex: An Adventure Survival Horror Story
   Depictions of whaling, cannibalism, homophobia, mention of harmful and inaccurate historical stereotypes of Native people

www.ingramcontent.com/pod-product-compliance
Lightning Source LLC
Chambersburg PA
CBHW011526211224
19375CB00024B/1560